This was what it \[...\] thought, to have a woman not just to sleep with but to hold.

The awkwardness eased and they sat there quietly. When she pushed away he felt the tug of regret.

"Sorry about that," she said.

He wasn't sorry, but how could he say so?

"That's okay. Happens sometimes." It never happened, actually.

She stared up at him and, bang, there it was again— that ache in his chest and the zing of attraction that crackled like the glass glaze Mrs. Yeager used on her white pots. Ray dropped his arm from her shoulder down to her waist.

"Oh," she said. Morgan inched away and met the resistance of his arm as he tightened his hold.

"My daughter is in the other room," she said.

That broke his concentration. His arm fell away and Morgan rose to her feet. She backed toward the door, pausing just inside the threshold with one hand on the doorknob, as if preparing to slam it shut and flee. It was the kind of chase he'd enjoy, but only if she would, too.

EAGLE WARRIOR

JENNA KERNAN

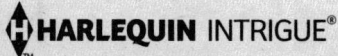

For Jim, always

Recycling programs
for this product may
not exist in your area.

ISBN-13: 978-0-373-75658-2

Eagle Warrior

Printed in U.S.A.

Jenna Kernan has penned over two dozen novels and has received two RITA® Award nominations. Jenna is every bit as adventurous as her heroines. Her hobbies include recreational gold prospecting, scuba diving and gem hunting. Jenna grew up in the Catskills and currently lives in the Hudson Valley of New York State with her husband. Follow Jenna on Twitter, @jennakernan, on Facebook or at jennakernan.com.

Books by Jenna Kernan

Harlequin Intrigue

Apache Protectors: Tribal Thunder

Turquoise Guardian
Eagle Warrior

Apache Protectors

Shadow Wolf
Hunter Moon
Tribal Law
Native Born

Harlequin Historical

Gold Rush Groom
The Texas Ranger's Daughter
Wild West Christmas
A Family for the Rancher
Running Wolf

Harlequin Nocturne

Dream Stalker
Ghost Stalker
Soul Whisperer
Beauty's Beast
The Vampire's Wolf
The Shifter's Choice

Visit the Author Profile page at Harlequin.com for more titles.

CAST OF CHARACTERS

Ray Strong—A Turquoise Guardian of Tribal Thunder, former US Marine and hotshot with a reputation for making bad choices.

Morgan Hooke—Daughter of the shooter who killed the mass gunman of the Lilac Mine.

Jack Bear Den—A detective with the tribal police and a Turquoise Guardian.

Carter Bear Den—Jack's twin brother, also a Turquoise Guardian and currently a protected witness.

Kenshaw Little Falcon—The head of the Turquoise Guardian medicine society, the tribe's medicine man and a spiritual leader with strong ties to community, tradition and the land.

Dylan Tehauno—A Turquoise Guardian, fellow hotshot and former US Marine with many commendations and honors.

Jefferson Rowe—Chief of police in the larger neighboring community of Darabee.

Theron Wrangler—Documentary filmmaker, environmentalist and the last person called by one of the men killed by the Lilac Mine shooter.

Guy Heron—Neighbor of Morgan's and friend of her father.

Luke Forrest—Black Mountain Apache and FBI agent in charge of investigating the Lilac Mine slaying.

Renzo Journey—Known member of the ecoextremist group WOLF.

Gifford Journey—Renzo's son and protector.

Chapter One

Most folks wouldn't trust Ray Strong to look after a houseplant let alone a woman and a child. But that was exactly what had happened. Ray watched the woman in question as she served a complimentary drink to one of the customers on the floor of the tribe's casino—she dipped as she set down the glass to avoid showing too much leg in her skimpy skirt. A shame, really, because she had great legs.

Detective Jack Bear Den, one of his friends and a fellow member of the warrior sect of the Turquoise Guardians medicine society, told him that they had all gone to high school with Morgan Hooke. But honestly, even after observing her several times over the past five days, Ray didn't remember her. That meant that she did not look like this back then.

Morgan was not beautiful, but compelling in a waifish sort of way. She had dark cautious eyes and a generous mouth. For reasons unknown, her thick shock of black hair was cut short on the sides and back and long on the top in a style favored by adolescent boys. He liked that cut on some actresses. But Morgan's hair lacked the product to make it look sassy, so it fell thick and straight in a bowl haircut that looked practical but not sexy, unless you noticed the long curve of her neck. Which he did, and that slim column of sensitive flesh gave him all kinds of bad ideas.

Some of the servers had released their top few buttons to reveal more of their breasts. But not Morgan. She wore the uniform in as conservative a manner as possible. Judging from her tip glass, he was not the only man in the room that rewarded less clothing and more skin.

He watched her retreat to the bar for more drinks. She did look good walking away. Not that it mattered. Ray was not here to pick Morgan up. An outsider had been asking about the shooter's daughter. The Anglo had even been at the casino last Sunday, Morgan's day off. A coworker had furnished Morgan's name, but not where she lived and the stranger had vanished. The woman had called their shaman, Kenshaw Little Falcon, who shared her concern, so he'd sent Ray to watch Morgan's back and see what she knew about her father's involvement in the crime. His shaman had been very specific. Keep her safe and find out if she knew who hired her father. Kenshaw believed that her father had not acted out of some need for justice but had been paid to shoot Ovidio Natal Sanchez. Why was obvious. But who—now that one was a puzzle.

Not as big a puzzle as why his shaman had chosen him for this job. Real dark horse he was and he knew it.

Morgan finished her shift and Ray trailed her out to the parking lot. Morgan stopped to pick up milk and processed cheese. Ray took the opportunity to buy beer and pork rinds. She didn't notice him. She never did because she kept her shoulders rounded and head down all the time. He didn't like it, wanted to shout at her to stand up straight.

Ray gazed across the space that separated them. She didn't seem the type for secrets. But she had at least one. No one seemed to know who fathered her child, Lisa. Everyone had secrets. That made it hard to tell about a person from what you saw on the outside. And no one ever got a look at the inside.

Next Morgan drove home to the small house that she had shared with her father and still shared with her ten-year-old girl. No sign of a man in her life though. A shame. She seemed fragile and Ray wondered why no man had responded to the compulsion to look after her. Not that he was that sort. Not at all.

She stopped again at the neighbor's to pick up Lisa. Her daughter was as skinny as a split rail with hair that flew out behind her when she ran, which she did often. In her features was the promise of beauty and none of the slinking posture her mother adopted. Lisa was bright-eyed and curious. She'd made eye contact with Ray a time or two and even thrown him a generous smile. He liked her. She was outgoing and a little crazy like him, judging from the way she climbed and swung and jumped on the playground at school during recess. But today was Saturday so no school.

When Morgan reached her dark and empty house, Ray waited on the road as Lisa charged toward the door.

April in the Arizona mountains meant that Lisa still wore a heavy coat, though it flapped open as she ran. Ray lifted his field glasses. He had the house behind hers. But this spot on the road gave him a better view of the kitchen. She never shut the curtains over the sink, so he could peer right in as she made dinner.

From his place on the shoulder, he could see both the kitchen on the front corner and one side of the house, including the back window where Morgan's father's bedroom was located. He caught the flash of movement in the bedroom. She left the shades up during the day; he suspected she did this for her cat, who liked sitting in that sunny window on the back of a worn upholstered chair.

Seeing a man pass the window, Ray shifted the direction of his gaze. Redirecting his field glasses, he saw that the contents of the room had been tossed about and there was someone searching the bookcase.

An instant later, Ray was out of his truck and running for the house.

Chapter Two

Morgan Hooke unlocked the front door and her daughter, Lisa, charged inside. One step took Morgan to the small rug just beyond the threshold. She exhaled, glad to finally be home. The day shifts were long and the guests were older, drank only the complimentary beverages and tipped almost nothing. Night shifts paid better, but without her father here at home, she needed to look after Lisa. That meant fewer hours and less pay. She'd picked up the Saturday hours only because a friend agreed to watch Lisa. Money had always been tight, but it had become stretched like the head of a war drum since her father's arrest.

Morgan flicked on the light, chasing off the late-day gloom and looked to the recliner where the cat usually slept. Finding the cushion empty, she scanned the tiny room for Cookie, the cat Lisa had dragged out of a Dumpster behind the school when it was only a kitten.

Lisa had tossed her backpack by the door and now called a greeting to her pet as she entered the eat-in kitchen and switched on the light. Cookie was usually there to greet them, meowing loudly for dinner. Morgan kicked off her shoes, retrieved Lisa's empty lunch bag from her backpack and carried both pack and bag into the kitchen. Lisa had already dropped the sack of groceries on the dinette before making her way down the hall that led to their three small bedrooms on her hunt for the gray cat with the startlingly green eyes.

Morgan frowned at the first prickling of unease. She hoped Cookie was all right because a vet visit was not in the budget.

"Cookie! Coook-key!"

Lisa sang the name and then made a familiar sound proven to lure the cat. The only noise Cookie responded to with greater frequency was that of the electric can opener.

"Mom!"

The alarm in Lisa's voice brought Morgan around. She glanced down the hall where Lisa stood motionless with her hands lifted slightly from her sides as she stared into her grandfather's room.

"Lisa? What's wrong?" Morgan was already moving and had cleared half the distance separating them as she prayed that nothing had happened to Cookie. Then she saw it. Her father was in Phoenix awaiting trial. No one should be in his room. But his overturned dresser now blocked the door.

A small gray cat could not do that.

"Lisa, honey," she whispered as the dread flooded over her suddenly clammy skin. "Come here to me right now."

"But what happened to…" Lisa took one step forward and threw her hand over her mouth. Then she turned and ran.

Morgan did not ask what she had seen. She asked nothing as she grabbed her daughter's wrist and ran for the closest door on bare feet. She heard the footsteps pounding down the hall and pushed Lisa ahead.

"Hurry!"

They cleared the hall and Lisa nearly reached the kitchen door when someone grabbed Morgan by her hair and tugged so hard she saw stars.

Lisa turned back. "Mom!"

A low male voice growled in Morgan's ear. "Where's the money?"

"Run!" she shouted to Lisa.

But her daughter hesitated.

"Get help," she said.

That sent her daughter off. Lisa rounded the table as the kitchen door flew open. Another man stood on the back step. Lisa screamed as the man lifted her off the ground, spun her in a circle and set her behind him on the back step.

"Run," ordered Morgan. The last thing she saw was her daughter's wide dark eyes before her captor tugged her backward into the hall.

"Where is it?" he asked, punctuating his question with a little shake.

Morgan grabbed hold of his wrists and twisted to face her attacker. Then she punched him in the bicep as she'd been taught by her dad. The man released her. Morgan staggered back, right into the second man.

The next instant she was behind him as he continued toward her attacker.

She saw the wide shoulders and clenched fists. Short black hair, a dark hoodie and long legs clad in new blue jeans. The man beyond him was now on his feet.

There was nothing said between them but she could tell by the way that the second man stalked the first that these two were not comrades.

"Listen, buddy," said her attacker, holding his hands up.

He didn't get a chance to finish. Morgan winced at the cracking sound of a fist striking the man's face. Blood sprayed on the white paint and the school photos tacked up in the hall. Morgan balled a fist before her mouth to stifle a scream. From outside Lisa shouted her mother's name.

Her rescuer thumped her captor's head on the hall runner as Morgan turned and fled.

RAY THOUGHT HE should have dropped the guy when he stopped fighting but gave him just one more shot for making him blow his cover. He'd been happy watching Morgan and Lisa from a distance. Experience had told him that things looked better that way. Now they'd seen him and he'd have to come up with something.

Damn.

He released the limp intruder and noticed that the housebreaker was bleeding all over himself but more important he was bleeding on Morgan's hall runner. Ray knew women despised mud or blood on carpets.

Once on his feet, Ray gave the guy a poke with his boot and the guy's head lolled. He retrieved the man's wallet and drew out his license.

"Andrew Peck." Ray glanced from the image of the smiling well-dressed man to the bloody, slack-faced Anglo with the rapidly swelling nose.

"You live in Darabee. Right up the road," Ray said.

A little searching of the billfold yielded several business cards. Mr. Peck was a manager at the Darabee Community Savings. Home invasion seemed a strange thing for a bank manager to be doing. He clearly was not very good at B and E or at personal defense. Ray kept the business card and tossed the wallet back on Mr. Peck's rising and falling chest where it bounced to the ground at his side.

Ray made a call to Kenshaw Little Falcon, reporting in. Little Falcon was his shaman, his spiritual leader, the head of their medicine society and the man who had hand selected the warrior sect called Tribal Thunder. Ray was proud to be among the newest members of the elite group of two dozen Tonto Apache men all selected from within the larger medicine society known as the Turquoise Guardians. Tribal Thunder recruits came from the men who completed the rigorous warrior training required to be considered a candidate. The newest inductees also included his friends Dylan Tehauno and Jack and Carter Bear Den. Like him, all three men were former US Marines but only he had a criminal record and a stunning proclivity for screw-ups.

His shaman told him to contact Jack Bear Den, who was also a member of Tribal Thunder and, conveniently, a detective with the tribal police here on Turquoise Canyon Reservation.

Their tribe of Tonto Apache was small, only 950 members but large enough for a casino and a manmade recreational lake, thanks to the Skeleton Cliff Damn. Their tribal police force totaled seven, including their dispatcher.

When he finished with Jack, he moved to the open back door to call to Morgan and Lisa. They didn't reply. The night was closing in but he could see that Morgan had them both locked in her car. Pitiful place to hide as he could break the glass with any number of rocks lying nearby, but at least he'd found them. She'd obviously left her keys inside the house.

He shouted to her that the police were coming and to stay put. Then he went to check out the damage the guy had done inside. He stepped over Mr. Peck to find a huge mess in the bedroom that had recently been occupied by Morgan's father. The mattress lay askew, bedding stripped, dresser drawers all emptied out.

Ray looked back at the intruder. "Aren't you ashamed of yourself?"

A glance in Lisa's and Morgan's rooms showed the man had either not looked there yet or chosen to focus on Karl's room.

Her father, Karl Hutton Hooke, had shot and killed the mass murderer who'd killed nine people down at the Lilac Copper Mine near the border last February. Ovidio Natal Sanchez had been apprehended in the town right outside the reservation boundary. On the very day the suspect had been delivered into custody, Mr. Hooke had walked right up and shot Sanchez twice through the heart. Nobody could explain why Karl had done it and, according to Jack, Morgan's dad refused to speak to anyone, including his court-appointed attorney.

Ray heard a sound in the hall and returned to find his captive make a failed attempt to rise.

"What were you looking for, Peck?"

Peck groaned and rolled his head from one side to the other. His hand went to his nose. He coughed blood and opened one eye.

"You want to tell me why you're here?" asked Ray.

"Do I know you?" Peck tried to staunch the copious amounts of blood issuing from his nose with his index finger and thumb. This forced the blood in a new direction and he began to cough.

"We only just met. Why are you here?"

"I was just…" His eyes shifted toward the kitchen, judging the distance to freedom and finding it too far. "I…it…"

"Yes?" Ray asked, lifting his brows and affecting a look of interest.

"I'm not saying a thing without a lawyer."

Ray smiled. "You have me confused with a law-abiding citizen. So let me explain." Ray squatted on his haunches and grabbed Mr. Peck, lifting him by the front of his bloody shirt. "I'm Apache and on *my* reservation." Ray showed him his empty hand. "I could kill you with this.

"Plus I have a criminal record and a bad temper. I'm not calling you a lawyer. So once again. Why, Mr. Peck, are you lying in Miss Hooke's hallway?"

Mr. Peck started to cry. "Please. You got to let me go."

Ray sighed and then shook his head. "No. I don't."

"I can pay you."

"Pay me?" Ray snorted. "This lady is a friend of mine. You scared her. So it's gone past money." Ray lifted Andrew's index finger and gave it a shake. "I expect a bank manager needs these."

Peck tried and failed to recover his hand with a weak tug. When he reached with his opposite hand Ray slapped him in the forehead with the heel of one hand. Peck's head thumped on the carpet and his hand fell away.

"I'm about to break this. Fair warning."

"All right. I was looking for the money."

The obvious question was what money, but Ray didn't do obvious.

"Yeah. Me, too. Why do you think it's here?"

Andrew's mouth quirked and a little of the fear left his expression. His pale twitchy eyes reminded Ray of a rodent.

"He didn't have much time between when he cashed the check and shot that man. Maybe twenty-four hours." He pointed toward the kitchen.

"She doesn't seem to have it. Or she's real smart. So I figured I'd start here."

"And you chose a time when Ms. Hooke would find you. Why?"

"No. I thought she worked nights at the casino. Somebody at the bank said so."

"She did. But her father used to watch her daughter. Now she's alone so…"

Andrew absorbed that. "Oh, yeah. Right. So what do you say? Fifty-fifty?"

"How much we talking here, Andy?"

His mouth clamped shut and he sniffed. Ray selected which digit to break and Peck writhed and whined.

"Okay. Okay. It was two hundred thousand. A bank check. He asked for cash. We had to make him come back. I don't keep that much on hand. So he came back, you know, the next day and the check was good. So I cashed it. And he walked right out of there with that money in a cardboard box. Just folded over the top flaps and tucked it under his arm."

Two hundred thousand? No wonder Kenshaw Little Falcon thought Morgan and her girl needed protection.

"You cleared the check?" asked Ray.

Peck nodded. "Sure did, after the bank in Phoenix cleared the funds."

How long had this twerp been watching Morgan, Ray wondered.

"Karl went away two months ago. Why now?" asked Ray.

"Because people are asking questions now. They're after it, the money. So, I thought I'd better get moving. I'd asked Ms. Hooke personally on two separate occasions when she came into the bank if she needed help investing. She declined. Seemed kind of puzzled. I think she's got it tucked in a mattress or something." Peck coughed blood and sniffed. "Say, mind if I sit down?"

Ray ignored the request. "What people?"

"A detective from Darabee came back in February, the one that got shot."

"Eli Casey?"

"Yes, so I figured he was out of the picture. But then a man came right to my church last Sunday morning and right during fellowship hour he asked me if I was the one who cashed the check for Karl in the amount of two hundred thousand dollars. I was so shocked I said, yes." Peck moved his hand and sniffed. Blood continued to flow down his face and neck. "Can I get a paper towel or some ice?"

"No. Who was he, the one from church?"

"I never saw him before. He didn't give me his name."

"You tell him anything else?"

"I may have said that the daughter's name was Morgan and she worked nights at the tribe's casino."

Last Sunday, Ray thought, the day before Kenshaw called him in to watch Morgan.

The sound of sirens reached him, still a ways off. He turned his head and then looked back at Peck, noting the moment he heard the approaching police.

"You called the cops?"

"You're trespassing on sovereign land."

"What about our deal?"

"Only deal I'll make is that if I ever see you on tribal land again, I'll break this." He set Peck's hand on his chest and gave it a little pat. "And, if I see you near Morgan or Lisa Hooke again, I'll kill you."

Peck trembled. Somehow the man sensed Ray wasn't bluffing. He was surprised to recognize that he wasn't making idle threats. He knew himself capable of killing this man for daring to touch Morgan. Why did this woman rouse every protective instinct in Ray's body? That question troubled him more than this miserable excuse for a burglar.

And who was the man at the casino asking questions? Ray set his teeth as he realized the threat to Morgan may have only just begun.

Chapter Three

Peck's eyes widened. As Ray stood over him, the bank manager rose to his elbows.

"You want it for yourself. Did you find it already? Is it gone?"

"Yeah. Gone." Ray made an exploding motion with both hands.

Ray left him to meet the police, passing Morgan and Lisa still sitting in the shabby white Honda with the windows rolled up and fogging. He noticed the gray duct tape securing the driver's side mirror and shook his head. She needed someone to look after her.

Morgan looked up at him with big wide eyes and in that moment she didn't look much older than her ten-year-old. He wondered two things simultaneously. How old had she been when she'd had Lisa and who was the bastard who left her all alone?

He gave Morgan a smile as he passed and belatedly noticed he had a bloody hoodie.

He knew the young officer who'd arrived first and directed him to the intruder. The next one he sent to speak to Morgan and Lisa.

"Tell her I'm her neighbor. I live right there." He pointed at the house behind hers.

"I thought you lived in Pinyon Forks," said Officer Cox.

"Looking after a friend's place for a few days while he's away."

Ray waited a few minutes for Jack to arrive. It didn't take long to tell him what he'd learned.

"He might press charges," said Jack.

Ray shrugged and made a hissing sound of dismissal. "So?"

Jack left it at that. He spoke to Morgan and her girl and oversaw the removal of the crying mess that Andrew Peck had become as his dreams of riches turned to the real possibility of jail time.

Peck went into a police unit and Jack waved Ray over to make introductions. Morgan stood with an arm resting protectively on her daughter's narrow shoulders. Lisa stayed close and very still, watching them.

"Ms. Hooke, this is an old friend of mine, Ray Strong. Ray and I served together in Iraq. I'm sure you have met him at some point. We were only a year ahead of you in school."

Jack didn't mention that Ray had dropped out and had to take his GED in order to join up with Carter, Dylan, Jack and Hatch.

The awkward pause coupled with Jack's scowl made Ray realize that Jack wanted him to chime in.

"Oh, yeah," said Ray. "Nice to see you again, Morgan. Long time." He rubbed his neck and glanced to Jack who lifted his chin as if silently ordering him to continue. Ray hated small talk. "I'm staying in Felix's place while he's away."

Morgan's expression brightened and she glanced toward her neighbor's house.

"Felix Potts? He told me he was going to Waco to visit his daughter and the new baby. It's her third."

Her voice was musical, like a flute, full of light air and sweet tones.

"Oh, yeah," said Ray, his skin prickling now. "Isn't that something?"

Ray's customary position with women was that they either turned him on or they didn't. If they did and they liked men with a bad reputation, and a surprising number did like that, then they were off to the races. Now he found himself in the awkward position of having to chat with a woman he had no intention of sleeping with.

He knew enough to stay clear of single mothers for a lot of valid reasons. And beyond that, it was a bad idea to mix work and play.

"He didn't tell me you'd be watching the place," said Morgan.

Because Kenshaw had called Potts after he'd left to ask if a fellow Turquoise Guardian could stay in his place. The answer, of course, was yes.

"Well, I'm watching it but he's helping me out. I lost my place recently so..." He looked to Jack to take over. Because he was terrible at making stuff up. Not at lying, he was very good at lying, convincing to a fault.

Morgan held her smile and she now did look beautiful. The pause stretched and her smile faded.

"Ray is a hotshot," said Jack. "One of our captains."

Morgan looked impressed and well she should. Their forest-fighting team was nationally recognized and much requested. They flew all over the country battling blazes. Seemed the Apache men were good at fighting anything, including fires.

Morgan gave Ray a long, speculative look and he could almost feel her gaze like a caress. His skin tingled and his palms began to itch. That wasn't good. Now he was staring at her mouth and *his* gaze had become speculative. Her lips and cheeks seemed especially pink.

She cleared her throat and he met her curious

expression with a grin. That grin had gotten him into more trouble than his fists. Her brows lifted as if reading the vibe he was sending and not knowing what to do with it.

"He'll be back next week. Will you be staying on when he comes home?" asked Morgan.

Ray squinted, wondering how to play this. "I need to find a place. I'm looking around."

Her gaze swept over him and he wished they were alone. He thought of Morgan's bed and imagined her stretched out naked on that the white coverlet. Clearly the sexual part of his brain had re-emerged. He shifted his position at the unwelcome ache that began below his belt.

"You were in the casino today," she said.

And yesterday and the day before that, he thought.

"Guilty," he said.

"Did I get you a drink?" she asked.

"No. I just come in to watch…"

Her frown deepened.

He grinned wider. "To watch the games on the big screens."

"Oh!" Her cheeks went bright pink.

Shame on her for making assumptions, he thought.

"Baseball," she said and smiled, the tension easing out of her shoulders.

Her daughter wiggled out from beneath her

mother's arm to take a step closer to Jack. She was staring up at the detective who was six-five in his stocking feet and now wore boots. If she didn't quit she'd get a crick in her neck.

"Are you Apache?" she asked him.

Ray's gaze shifted to Jack whose mouth went tight. Most folks didn't come right out and ask, but Lisa was ten and ten-year-olds were as blunt as dull axes.

"Yeah. Sure am. Roadrunner Clan. You?"

Lisa was still eying the mountain of a man that Jack had become. He looked more Samoan than Apache and it was a constant sore spot for Jack.

"I'm Butterfly Clan," said Lisa. "Why was that man in our house?"

Ray watched Morgan to see what her reaction might be and found her looking as curious as Lisa. Had working in that casino taught her to bluff or was she in the dark?

Was it possible that her father had not told her about the money?

He had other questions, chief of which was what in the wide world had Karl Hutton Hooke done to receive a bank check for two hundred thousand dollars with his name written on it?

The answer seemed obvious. Her father had been paid to kill the Lilac Copper Mine Gunman. That meant that Karl Hutton Hooke was a hitman and whoever paid him had not wanted the mass gunman to stand trial. It also meant that there was a whole mess of money missing.

Jack escorted Morgan back inside and together they checked the house. Only her father's room had been disturbed, but Andy had even gone so far as to slice the pillows and mattress.

"What a mess," Ray said from the doorway.

Morgan directed her question to Jack. "What was he looking for, Detective Bear Den?"

Chapter Four

"Not sure what he was looking for, Morgan," said Detective Bear Den. "Did your dad have anything of special value?"

Both Jack and Ray watched Morgan who seemed to be considering the question while lightly rubbing her fingertips over her lips. The small gesture sent an unexpected shot of longing straight to Ray's groin.

He lifted his brows in surprise. He didn't go for this sort of woman, the "attached with child, daughter of a murderer who might be involved with some very bad people" sort. But there it was, Ray Strong making the worst possible choice, as usual.

His attention now became speculative. What kind of a woman was Morgan in bed?

"He had some of those state quarters," said Morgan. "Turquoise jewelry. Not a lot."

She convinced Ray. If he was a betting man,

and of course, he was, he would say dear old Dad had forgotten to tell his girl that he'd had a payday that might just get her and her daughter killed.

They all moved inside and gathered in the kitchen in a loose circle between the dinette and the worn Formica counters.

"You have somewhere you can stay tonight?" asked Jack.

Morgan drew Lisa in beside her, and her daughter hugged her mom around the middle. Morgan stood in bare feet still wearing the cocktail outfit that looked garish in the drab little kitchen.

"Lisa could stay at her best friend's. The Herons live right next door. But I...I think I'd better stay here."

"You have someone to call, maybe help you clean up?" asked Jack.

"I can help," said Ray.

Morgan's face scrunched up in a way that told Ray that he was less than smooth in her eyes.

"That's not necessary," she said, her smile all tight and dismissive now. That made Ray want to remind her who had removed the vermin from her house.

"I'll have an officer escort you and Lisa to the Herons'," said Jack.

Jack left them and called from the door into the yard. Ray clasped his bloody hands behind his back and gave Morgan a half smile that he hoped made him look less threatening. Jack returned with a young man that Ray knew.

"Ms. Hooke, this is Officer Wetselline," said Jack, sounding all professional now. "He'll walk you over to the Herons'. Maybe you want to wait over there until we finish up here."

She nodded her head and took hold of Lisa's hand. "I'll be back."

Ray watched Morgan go and wondered what she'd look like in tight jeans and a thin white T-shirt. Ever since he'd started watching her, he couldn't stop these images from creeping into his mind. Why her? He didn't date women with children but he liked Lisa and Morgan had the sort of appeal that seemed deeper than physical. She was such a dedicated mom and supportive daughter. Many women would have distanced themselves from a father who committed such a reprehensible act. Not her. According to Kenshaw, she visited her father, often. Respectable, upstanding, devoted, yeah…not his type.

Jack snapped his fingers in front of Ray's face, bringing his attention away from Morgan. Jack filled Ray in on his conversation with their shaman.

"He wants you here on site with Ms. Hooke."

"What? How am I supposed to pull that off?" asked Ray.

"I'm going to suggest Morgan not be alone.

That her father's arrest might have repercussions for her and Lisa."

"You're not going to tell her about the money?"

"You said that Peck asked her about the money," said Jack.

"That's the first thing I heard when I came in. But she thinks we're talking about state quarters." The image of Morgan being dragged backward by that cowardly little branch manager made Ray want to punch him in the face all over again.

"I can ask her a second time, suggest that her father might have some additional money."

"Don't suggest. Tell her the truth. Her father might have been paid to shoot Ovidio Sanchez. He cashed a huge check the day before he went to jail and that pecker Peck was in her home, looking for the loot."

"This could be very dangerous for her. So I'm going to recommend strongly that she consider hiring a bodyguard. Then I'm putting your hat in the ring."

"I'm no bodyguard."

Jack seemed to know where his mind was going. "You couldn't get to him, Ray. There wasn't time."

Ray never missed a beat as he skipped to Iraq and the night that none of them would ever forget.

"But I could have let him ride with Mullins. Mullins wanted him. But I stuck him with

Tromgartner." The prank had not been funny. Instead it had cost his best friend his life. If only that had been all.

"I didn't get to them either," said Jack. In fact, Jack had held Ray back and let go only to grab his brother Carter. Then he'd run them both out leaving Hatch behind.

Ray blew out a breath. Jack scratched at the stubble on his jaw and smoothly changed the subject.

"She doesn't seem to know anything about the money."

"Who knows what she knows," said Ray. You would think a detective would be more suspicious.

"Let me talk to her when she gets back and you wash the blood off your hands."

"This is a mistake. Kenshaw should call Dylan Tehauno. He's clean-cut, responsible. And he's not crazy. That's for sure."

"Maybe she needs crazy to protect her from bigger crazy."

Ray sighed. He'd never felt less prepared for a job.

"One thing I know," said Jack. "Morgan Hooke will be in danger until that money is found."

Ray couldn't dispute that because it was true. Her father had made a mistake going to a bank so close to home. Maybe it didn't matter. That kind of money would bring trouble even if trouble had to travel long distances.

"Fox guarding the hen house," muttered Ray.

"Yeah, well that hen got plucked a long time ago."

Ray was interested in this conversation. "Who?"

"Don't know. No rumors even."

Ray frowned. In a small place like this, there were always rumors. "See if you can find out."

"Because?" asked Jack.

"Because I'm curious, is all."

Jack raised his eyebrows. "Really?"

He sounded so shocked it pissed Ray right off. "Yeah."

"Not your type, Ray."

"I know that, Jack."

"Fine, I'll see what I can find out."

Jack followed his officer, leaving Ray in Karl Hooke's empty bedroom. Ray ducked into the bathroom to wash his hands and then returned to set Karl's room in order. First, he righted the dresser. Jack returned as Ray was sliding the mattress back in place.

"Where would you put it?" asked Jack.

"Not in the room beside where my granddaughter slept." As if he'd ever have a granddaughter, Ray thought, which he wouldn't. He was actually shocked he'd lived this long.

"You think Kenshaw knows?" asked Jack.

The two shared a hard look. He understood what Jack was asking. Detective Jack Bear Den wondered if their shaman knew about the money when tribal law enforcement did not. Ray knew Kenshaw had some information because he'd asked Ray to find out if Morgan knew who hired her dad. That meant Kenshaw either knew or suspected that Morgan's dad did not act of his own volition. Did Kenshaw also know about the money?

Is that why his shaman had sent him? Was it more than a stranger's interest in Morgan that caused Kenshaw to send Ray to her? He couldn't send a detective to investigate this because Jack had an obligation to uphold the law and investigate crimes. Meanwhile Ray was blissfully free of such responsibility—any responsibility really, including taking care of houseplants.

"Don't jump to conclusions," said Ray. "Might be that Kenshaw saw Hooke make the withdrawal at the bank or Hooke contacted him to look after his girls."

Jack made a face. "Or maybe Carter was right."

Jack's twin brother, Carter, was currently in federal protection with his new wife, Amber Kitcheyan, who was Kenshaw Little Falcon's niece. They were witnesses in a federal case involving an eco-extremist group called WOLF. Carter had been sent by Little Falcon to deliver a message to their shaman's niece. As a result, his niece had survived the slaying that had killed everyone else in her office, and Jack's brother was now gone from the rez as the Feds prepared their case. Jack feared Carter might have to enter witness protection after the case settled because of possible threats from the extremists. Jack believed the timing of Carter's mission was evidence that their spiritual leader and head of their medicine society had foreknowledge of the mass slaying. If he did, Jack was obliged to arrest him.

"I'm back," called Morgan from the open doorway.

"Wait here," said Jack to Ray.

He did as he was told, setting the drawers back in the dresser and then piling the scattered clothing on the bed. He wondered about Morgan's father. He understood the need for a payday. But he did not understand risking his freedom and his daughter's life in the pursuit of money. Whether it had been his intention or not, Morgan's life was now in danger because Ray just knew that branch manager Andrew Peck was not the sort of man who could keep a secret. The minute he figured out he needed help to get his greedy mitts on the loot, he would tell someone—someone more competent and more dangerous.

More would come for the money and when they couldn't find it, they'd come after Morgan and her daughter. Their troubles were far from over and Ray wondered again if he was up to the task Kenshaw had set for him. Keeping Morgan safe just became a full-time gig.

Chapter Five

Morgan felt suddenly unsure about entering her own kitchen. Officer Wetselline had accompanied her from the Herons' home back here. And she knew her attacker was gone. But still her heart hammered as she stood poised to cross that threshold.

Flashes of the attack exploded like fireworks in her mind. Lisa's scream. Her own voice. *Run!* The man growling as he yanked her backward against his fleshy body. *Where is it?*

"Ma'am?" asked the young patrolman behind her.

She glanced back at him, enfolding herself in a hug and rubbing at the gooseflesh that lifted on her arm.

"Getting cold," she said, making excuses for her chattering teeth.

"Would you like me to walk you in?" he asked.

She smiled and was about to tell him that was

unnecessary, but her stomach tightened and she felt dizzy at just the thought of walking down that hallway.

"I'm fine," she lied. "Thank you."

His skeptical look told her she hadn't fooled him.

She glanced about the empty interior. Her daughter's checked nylon lunch bag sat on the counter with the sack of milk and groceries. The red-and-white soup can had rolled halfway across the dull surface. Otherwise everything looked normal. She stepped gingerly inside and felt the terror close in as she realized how close her daughter had been to the intruder. Her shoulders gave an involuntary shudder. She swallowed and then called out to Detective Bear Den.

"I'm back."

Morgan glanced out the door, past the officer to the lights of her neighbor's kitchen. She knew that Lisa was safe with Trish and Guy Heron. Her neighbors had naturally been concerned about the break-in, but she assured them that the guy had been caught and that she just needed to clean the place up before retrieving her daughter. They had been wonderful, as always. The Herons' daughter, Ami, was Lisa's best friend and the two of them had disappeared into Ami's room moments after their arrival.

Where is it?

The chill climbed up Morgan's neck.

Where was what? she wondered.

Ray Strong was nowhere in sight, but Detective Bear Den stepped out from the hallway and paused in the eat-in kitchen beside the oval table. His tread was light for such a big man. She had known him since elementary school when he had begun growing early and fast. Lord, he was big. She also remembered his brother, Carter, because his twin did not look a thing like Jack. None of the younger Bear Den boys had Jack's build or looks either. It had caused Jack trouble all his life.

She vaguely remembered that Ray Strong had been connected with something bad.

"How is Lisa?" asked the detective.

"Scared. But all right. What was he looking for?" she asked. *Where is it?* Was that voice going to haunt her dreams?

"What makes you think he was looking for something?"

"He broke in. Tossed things around in my father's room. I thought..." She stopped talking. Should she tell Bear Den what her attacker had asked?

"Have there been any repercussions from your father's involvement with Ovidio Sanchez?"

What a polite way to ask if her father assassinating the prime suspect in a mass slaying had affected them.

"Lisa has been having a hard time at school. Kids can be mean."

"And you?"

"I had to switch to days because Dad isn't here at night anymore." And her daughter had lost the only father she'd ever known and Morgan didn't understand why her father had done such a thing. It was like standing on the shore of a river only to discover that the water had undercut the bank. She and her daughter had tumbled and were still falling toward an uncertain future. Morgan knew that soon she would have to petition the tribe for assistance and the prospect shamed her. She didn't say any of that aloud, however, and only just managed to mutter that it had been hard.

Bear Den's brows dropped lower over his pale eyes. "I am asking if you have received any threats."

She shook her head. "No. Nothing like that."

"Did you know what your father was planning?"

"The police at Darabee already asked me that. I was interviewed over there."

"By Jefferson Rowe?"

"Who?"

"Police Chief Rowe?"

She shook her head. "I don't think so. A detective. I don't remember his name. He asked me if I knew beforehand, too. I didn't." And she felt stupid that she had noticed nothing unusual…and sad that her father had not confided in her and angry at what he had done. She glanced toward the door. "Have you seen a gray cat?"

"No."

She tried calling Cookie from the back door but with the strangers about and the flashing lights, she didn't expect to see the cat until things calmed down.

Her interruption did not distract the detective from his line of questioning.

"Did your father leave you anything? Instructions. A letter."

"Like a suicide note?" Morgan was still hugging herself. The April air turned cold at night in the mountains so she moved to close the kitchen door. Ray Strong anticipated her actions and got there first. Her hand brushed his before she could draw back. The contact was quick so she could not understand why her insides tightened and her breath caught. The door clicked and she met Ray's dark compelling eyes. One of his brows quirked.

Bear Den cleared his throat, snapping Morgan's attention back to the detective's question. Did she have foreknowledge of her father's plan to commit murder?

"He didn't say anything. The morning before the shooting he took his truck. He's not supposed to drive anymore. I was sleeping when he left. I get home from work about eight a.m. and Dad usually gets Lisa up and I get her ready for school. Then I usually sleep from nine to about three. He wasn't here when Lisa got off the bus but he was here before my shift. He wouldn't tell me where he had gone. The next day he…" She hesitated, tugging at her ear. This topic still made her feel nauseous and baffled all at once. "He left and afterward they arrested him in Darabee. I was waiting for Lisa's bus when tribal police and the FBI got here. They searched the house. They took some things. Maybe they found something like that."

"They didn't. Usually when someone is planning such a thing, they make preparations. Say goodbye."

She thought back to the evening before when she saw him last. "He asked me to pick up a chocolate cake."

Bear Den scowled. "Cake."

"He wanted cake. Gave me the money."

"What money?"

Now she scowled. "For the cake. I don't buy that junk and he shouldn't have it either. But I bought the cake and we had that after dinner on Thursday night for no reason." She stared at the detective. "Was that it? The cake? Like some kind of going away party?"

Jack Bear Den shook his head. "I don't know."

Morgan stared at her kitchen tiles and tried to keep from crying.

"Ms. Hooke, my friend Ray spoke to the guy who broke into your house. The man indicated he was searching for money. He said your father cashed a bank check for two hundred thousand dollars in Darabee."

She snorted at first, thinking he was kidding and then her jaw dropped open as she saw he was deadly serious.

"I have to report that to the FBI. So what I want to know from you is, did you know about this money?"

She couldn't even speak, so she shook her head.

"Do you know where the money currently is?"

"No." Her words were a whisper. "I don't. You think he actually had that much money?"

Jack nodded. "I believe your father was accepting payment."

"Payment? What could he possibly do that was worth that kind of…"

Morgan's knees buckled and Bear Den caught her, drew out a chair and guided her into it. Her fanny hit with enough force to jar her gaze to the detective.

"This can't be happening."

Bear Den looked down the hall. "Ray? Can you come out?"

Her protector emerged from the hall. The front

of his shirt was soaking wet and stuck to his chest, revealing the ripped muscles of his abdomen. Morgan's breath caught at the perfection of his form.

"Why are you all wet?" she asked.

Bear Den followed the direction of her gaze. Ray shrugged. "Washed off the blood."

The detective groaned and Morgan blinked, finally forcing her attention away, but took one more long look because a sight like that should be committed to memory.

Bear Den took a seat across from her and Ray retrieved the one between them, spun it and sat, his long legs straddling the back. Then he hugged the top and rested his chin on his hands. At least she couldn't see the wet spot or his tight abs any longer.

Bear Den cleared his throat. "I was just relaying what the intruder told you."

Ray's gaze flicked from the detective to her. "You have some problems, Morgan."

"What are you two implying exactly?"

Ray deferred to the detective.

"It appears that your father cashed a check twenty-four hours prior to his attack on the prime suspect in the Lilac Copper Mine shooting."

"I don't understand."

Ray tucked in his legs and lifted his chin from his hands. "Your father was a paid hitman. Now word is out about the payday, and that means you can expect more like that nitwit I found in your hallway."

Morgan's stomach heaved. She pressed a hand over her pounding heart.

"More."

"More and more competent."

"Competent?"

"Dangerous. The kind of men that don't pull hair. And they won't stop until you deliver that money."

"What money? I don't have it."

"Well I suggest you find it fast. The trick will be to keep you safe in the meantime."

She sat back in the chair. "How am I supposed to do that, exactly?"

"That's where I come in."

Morgan looked from Ray to Detective Bear Den.

"You need a bodyguard, Morgan. Someone tough, resourceful and capable of protecting you."

Her gaze flicked back to Ray Strong.

"Ray has agreed to act as your bodyguard," said Detective Bear Den.

He stood there watching her like a hungry wolf in his transparent T-shirt rippling with contained potency. He was just the sort of male to cause a woman all kinds of trouble.

"I can't afford to put gas in my car," Morgan said. "How am I going to pay for…" She let her traitorous eyes caress him and his mouth twitched. His eyes glittered as if he knew what she was thinking. "I couldn't afford to even feed him let alone pay him."

"You can't afford not to," said Bear Den.

Morgan regarded Ray Strong. The man was tough, powerful and had already shown himself capable of protecting her and Lisa. He also ignited in Morgan an unwelcome burst of lust coupled with a rational sense of fear. The man was dangerous and the threat he posed was more than physical.

She shook her head. "This is a bad idea."

Bear Den spoke again, his voice deep and resonant. "Are you familiar with the Turquoise Guardians?"

"My dad's medicine society? Sure."

"There is a sect within that organization called Tribal Thunder. This is a warrior band."

Morgan didn't think they still had warriors, not the real kind that defended their families to the death, made war on their enemies and took what they liked. She found her gaze slipping back to Ray like a thief on a night raid.

"I don't know of Tribal Thunder."

"Ray is a member of that sect. So am I. We've sworn an oath to defend our tribe."

Now Ray took up the conversation. His voice did funny things to her insides.

He thumbed over his shoulder at her closed back door. "That little twerp is going to spill his guts. Word will get out. There is no calling it back. If you won't do this for yourself, do it for your daughter."

Word will get out.

Lisa. Her gaze went to the back door. What had she caught while her mother was attacked? What had she overheard the officers say afterward and most importantly, what had she told their neighbors?

"I need to get Lisa back." Was that her voice? It didn't even sound like hers.

"I'll have one of my officers fetch her," said Jack.

"No!" Morgan headed out the door at a run and Ray caught her easily. He didn't grab her or try to stop her, just jogged along beside her across the dirt and gravel that separated her door from the Herons'.

She burst through the back door to find Guy Heron alone in the kitchen with Lisa. He had a hold of each of her daughter's shoulders. Every hair on Morgan's neck lifted. At seeing Morgan, his expression changed from eagerness to guilt. His gaze flashed from her to Ray Strong, now standing behind her. Now she saw fear.

"Oh, hey," said Guy. "Everything all right?"

Morgan glanced to Lisa. Her daughter looked

frightened and she did not need to call to her. Morgan just lifted a hand and Lisa ran to her mother. Their hands clasped and Morgan drew herself up as she tugged Lisa behind her.

"We were just talking about what happened tonight. Just your dad's room, huh?" Guy's voice held a note of force levity but the room had gone deadly quiet.

"Take Lisa home," said Ray.

Morgan turned to go and then paused as she recalled the man Ray had beaten in her house. She'd seen him dragged out by two officers. His face had been swollen, raw and bloody. Morgan glanced at Mr. Heron. The man had been interrogating her daughter. Morgan knew it and so did Mr. Strong. The fury and fear mingled into a hard lump in Morgan's stomach. Then she looked at Ray Strong, who had dipped his chin and fixed his gaze on Guy in a way that seemed like anticipation. The muscles at his neck bunched in coiled potential energy.

He tore his gaze from Guy to meet hers.

"You're hired, Mr. Strong."

Chapter Six

Ray returned to Morgan's kitchen to find Jack alone at the dinette taking notes on a notepad.

Ray's head swiveled. "Where's the girl?"

"Bedroom. Morgan's with her. Lisa was crying."

Ray's fists clenched and he considered taking Lisa's distress out on Mr. Heron.

"Everything okay?" asked Jack, lifting his chin in the direction of the neighbor.

"He's not bleeding, if that's what you're asking."

Ray briefly related the high points of his chat with her dorky, slimy neighbor.

"He knows from the girl that Karl had money. Not how much. But he's already put two and two together."

Ray hoped he had reached an understanding with Guy Heron. But in his experience, the one thing that trumped fear was greed.

"We're done here," said Jack. "You'll be staying in her father's room."

Appropriate, he thought because her father and he shared certain things. They were both Turquoise Guardians, Apache men and they both had a tendency to break the law. The downside of the room choice was that Karl had a big bed and it was right across the hall from the tempting Morgan Hooke.

"You staying while I get my kit?" asked Ray.

Jack nodded and laced the fingers of his massive hands on the dining room table.

"Be back as quick as I can."

RAY MOVED QUICKLY, scouting once around the perimeter before returning to Felix Potts's home to retrieve his belongings. He returned from Potts's house and moved his truck, parking prominently in the driveway beside Jack's tribal police SUV. Then he pulled his olive green gunnysack over one shoulder and lifted his small duffel, which held mostly weapons.

When he reached the kitchen stoop he was greeted by a gray cat that meowed loudly. Then it stood and rubbed against his leg.

"You live here, too?" he asked.

He rapped on the door and let himself in. The cat scooted past him.

He found Jack leaning with his back to the sink

beside Morgan who stood at the stove. The aroma of tomato soup and cooking macaroni greeted him. Morgan stopped stirring the contents of one pot and held the dripping spoon poised over it as she watched him drop his things beside the door, wipe his feet and step into the space. Maybe he should have knocked.

Jack pushed off the sink, which was good because Ray thought there was only one reason to stand that close to a woman. Jack was single. So was Morgan. It shouldn't have mattered because Morgan was a job and a burden, yet her boyish looks had unexpectedly hit him down low and deep. So it did matter.

He glared at Jack, who lifted his brows in surprise and moved out of the kitchen.

"Need any help?" asked Jack.

Ray shook his head.

"I'll check in tomorrow. Let you know what else we get from the bank manager."

Since Jack wasn't allowed to use his fists with the same liberty as Ray, he doubted he'd get much. Little dweebs like that always lawyered up.

Jack called a farewell to Lisa and then to Morgan.

"You're in good hands, Morgan. I'd trust Ray Strong with my life. You can do the same."

She thanked Jack with a sincerity that made Ray scowl all over again. He could see them together—naked. Ray rubbed his eyes. Jack shook his hand and headed out into the night. Ray locked the door behind him and found satisfaction in the click.

The cat rubbed against his leg and meowed loudly again.

"What?" Ray asked it. "If you want food you're at the wrong human."

"Cookie!" Morgan ran to the feline and lifted the boneless ball of fluff. "Where did you find her? Lisa will be so happy."

In Ray's experience cats never needed finding. Morgan squeezed the cat, which now hung over her shoulder, its green eyes watching Ray. Morgan carried the cat to Lisa's room and was met with squeals of delight from the interior. When Morgan came back, her smile eased away at the sight of him still in her kitchen.

"How's your girl?" asked Ray.

"Better now that she has Cookie." Her smile was so sweet and so compelling, Ray took a step toward her before he realized he had moved.

"Detective Bear Den said that you would work for room and board as a favor to my father." He'd work for nothing, but staying on site would make it much easier to guard Lisa and Morgan.

Morgan poured the macaroni into a colander in the sink, sending steam billowing upward.

If Morgan Hooke knew the location of the two

hundred thousand dollars, would she be eating condensed soup for dinner?

"And on behalf of your medicine society."

He nodded and tugged at his drying shirt, wishing he could avoid this chatting.

"Tribal Thunder," said Morgan. "I never heard of that sect."

He really could not speak of his medicine society with a woman, even an Apache woman like Morgan. But he did say that it was a warrior sect.

"We've vowed to protect the sovereignty of our heritage, resources and tribe."

"And I fall under tribe," she said, flipping on the hot water and engaging the sprayer to give the limp pasta a shower. Deftly she dumped the noodles back into the pot, added milk, butter and the envelope of fluorescent yellow cheese-like product. Then the pot went back on the stove on a low flame.

"I added another box because—" she waved a clean wooden spoon at him "—you look hungry."

Wow, she shouldn't have said that. He stepped closer. Her eyes rounded. He closed in on an impulse so strong he didn't even question it.

He wrapped her up and found that slippery cocktail dress made her glide up his chest as if she wore satin. When he angled his head to kiss her she pointed the clean end of the wooden spoon into his chest like the butt end of a nightstick.

The mac and cheese was sizzling as the milk boiled away.

"Bad idea," she said, but then licked her wide lower lip, sending him mixed signals.

"That's what I'm best at."

She pulled away and he let her go.

They faced off.

"Listen, you might have some ideas about me because I have a child and no husband. And because I serve drinks. So let me set you straight. I'm not interested in casual sex."

"Great. Because sex is one of two things I take very seriously."

She lowered the spoon. "What's the other?"

"Protecting you and Lisa."

MORGAN STARED UP at her protector. He stood only an arm's length from her with his hand still resting on her shoulder. His face was clean-shaven, revealing the hard line of his jaw and his prominent chin. It looked like the kind of jaw that could take a punch and the kind of chin that dared you to try. He had tousled thick black hair that needed a trim and a wide square forehead with heavy brows. His brown eyes now seemed to hold a hint of green and shone with mischief. He wasn't done with her, they seemed to say. Not by a long shot. His mouth quirked, confirming her suspicion. The man was imposing as all get out, but right now that was what she needed. A man capable of taking care of things as well as her and her daughter.

Morgan understood the seriousness of her situation. It was bleeding into her consciousness like dye into fabric.

"You going to be able to do this?" she asked.

He never took his eyes off her as he nodded.

Ray Strong cocked his head, lifting a hand to trail his fingertips down the sensitive skin of her neck and on to the hollow at her throat. She shivered as sensation rocked her.

"I've been wanting to do that," he said.

His grin promised devilment.

Trouble.

"Mom?"

Chapter Seven

The man was a chameleon, Morgan thought.

Ray now stood at a respectable distance from Morgan, his powerful arms folded and his posture relaxed. Even his smile was different. His expression held none of the banked desire she'd witnessed. Instead she saw only a benign hint of a smile that made him seem, if not exactly safe, at least not imminently dangerous.

She cleared her throat and forced a tight smile. "Lisa honey, dinner is ready."

Lisa had halted on the bare floor where the carpet runner had been pausing at the place where hallway gave way to the worn floor tiles of the kitchen. The cat sat at her heels, tail tucked around its front feet. They both stared at Ray with curiosity. Lisa's eyes were focused on Ray as if seeing a rattlesnake coiled in her path and calculating her way clear. Her dark eyes seemed to assess a new potential threat. Her girl had more sense than her mother, thought Morgan.

"Lisa, this is Mr. Strong. He will be staying in Pop-Pop's room for a while."

"Why?"

While Morgan debated how much to tell her, Ray stepped forward as Lisa slid a foot backward, preparing to retreat.

"Because the man who broke in here was looking for something of your grandfather's. You have friends at school?"

Lisa nodded.

"Anyone ever have a big secret?"

Lisa nodded again.

"What happened to that secret?"

Lisa looked to her mother and then fixed her attention on Ray. "My friend told our other friend and she promised never, ever to tell, but she must have because I didn't tell and then Bobby Farrow knew and he told all the boys."

"Exactly."

He didn't draw the connection. Just waited. Morgan waited, too.

"So that man, the one who grabbed my mother, he's going to tell Pop-Pop's big secret?"

Ray nodded. "Smart girl."

Lisa's eyes widened in understanding. "And Mr. Heron. He knows because I told him that man asked Mom for the money."

"Yes."

"I shouldn't have said anything."

Morgan went to her daughter and brushed her thick black hair from her face. "It's all right, sweetheart."

Lisa kept her attention on Ray.

"How did you know that the man would hurt us?"

"I didn't. But I've been watching over you two for a while now."

That made Morgan's attention snap from her child to Ray. How long had he been watching them?

"I've seen you at the store and other places."

Ray nodded. "That's right. I got asked by a friend of your grandfather's to watch over you and your mama."

"Do you know the secret?"

"Just that it's about money. Hidden money."

Morgan didn't think Lisa should know that. Didn't want her at risk. But she was at risk, whether she knew or not.

"It's here?" asked Lisa.

"Nobody knows where."

"Except Pop-Pop, so let's go ask him."

Ray glanced back at her and Morgan nodded. That was the logical next step.

"Tomorrow," said Morgan, knowing there were visiting hours then. "Wash up. Dinner is ready."

Lisa moved to the kitchen sink and washed her hands. Morgan eyed him and he followed Lisa, but he had already washed his hands when he'd removed her intruder's blood. Morgan fed the cat some mush from a can. Cookie, apparently, ate first.

They sat down to a meal of tomato soup with mac and cheese. Ray finished his portion and glanced around for more, finding the only remaining pasta on Lisa's plate. He glanced at Morgan who shot him a stern look. She was such a fierce feisty woman it made him smile.

After supper, Lisa drew out her school books and mother and daughter sat together. Morgan read the paper and helped Lisa as needed. Ray took the opportunity to bring his things into Karl's room and to peer out all the windows on the back of the house.

He heard someone enter the room and turned to see Morgan standing with a mound of folded sheets in her arms.

"I thought I'd change these," she said, lifting her arms slightly to indicate the linen.

"Thanks." He stripped off the lovely Pendleton wool blanket that had bold black stripes on a field of red and had the top sheet off before she reached the bed.

"I can do this," she said.

"So can I. I was in the US Marines for a while.

One thing I learned was how to make my bed." He'd also perfected his aim with a rifle and handgun. Ray had already known a thing or two about hand-to-hand combat and had more practical experience tracking than most men gleaned in a lifetime.

"My father fought in Vietnam."

Ray knew that. He'd shared a few stories with Karl at their medicine society.

"Sharpshooter," said Ray.

Morgan's jaw dropped but she recovered. "That's right."

She pulled free two corners of the fitted sheet and he released the corners on his side. Morgan began replacing the linen and Ray worked on the two pillowcases. They worked in silence with a fluidity that made their motions seem almost like a dance. They leaned over the bed from opposite sides to place the pillows and their eyes met. Morgan flushed so Ray guessed she was thinking of him stretched out on these clean white sheets… alone…possibly naked.

She straightened and threw out the top sheet so that it fluttered to his side. The blanket followed. She placed a clean sage-green towel on the foot of the bed.

"There. You're all set."

"Thank you again. And for letting me stay."

"I have great respect for Kenshaw Little Falcon

and for my father, despite what he has done." She sat on the bed, her hands splayed on the red wool, her shoulders slumped again in that whipped-dog posture he despised. She glanced up at him. "Do you think people deserve second chances, Mr. Strong?"

He sat beside her. "I've already tried to kiss you, Morgan. I think you should call me Ray."

He wanted to try again.

"Fine. Ray. My father killed a man. Probably for money. I can't get my mind around that."

He'd killed more than one man, Ray knew. More than Ray had killed. Karl had been very good at his assignment in Vietnam.

"I can think of two reasons he might want to earn money."

She looked at him. "You mean me and Lisa. I would much prefer to have my father here with us. You might not believe this, but he was wonderful with Lisa. Very kind and patient. He's been with her since she was born, more a father to her than a grandfather, and she doesn't understand any more than I do why he would do such a thing."

"We'll ask him tomorrow."

Her sigh was heavy and Ray felt an unexpected urge to comfort her. That wasn't his forte, holding women who were wearing their clothing. But he wrapped an arm around her and tried to ignore the flowery fragrance of her hair. It took a few moments and his remembering being rocked back to sleep by Mrs. Yeager during one particularly vivid nightmare, but he finally remembered a long-forgotten skill, one he'd learned without realizing. Comfort was not something that women came to him for. Never before, actually, but Morgan hadn't come to him. He'd been forced on her. He had to remember that.

She sagged against him and rested her head on the hollow between his shoulder and collarbone. Funny, the rocking and the warmth of her little body against him made him close his eyes to savor the sensations. And suddenly she was comforting him.

This was what it must be like, he thought, to have a woman not just to sleep with but to hold. The awkwardness eased and they sat there quietly. When she pushed away he felt the tug of regret.

"Sorry about that," she said.

He wasn't sorry but how could he say so?

"That's okay. Happens sometimes." It never happened, actually.

She stared up at him and, bang, there it was again, that ache in his chest and the zing of attraction that crackled. Ray dropped his arm from her shoulder and down to her waist.

"Oh," she said. Morgan inched away and met with the resistance of his arm as he tightened his hold.

"My daughter is in the other room," she said.

That broke his concentration. His arm fell away and Morgan rose to her feet, perhaps belatedly realizing it is always unwise to enter a tiger's cage even if it appears docile. She backed toward the door, pausing just inside the threshold with one hand on the doorknob, as if preparing to slam it shut and flee. It was the kind of chase he'd enjoy, but only if she would, too. He smiled as images of Morgan, playful and laughing, danced in his mind. They'd roll on the couch and onto the floor, where he'd let her sprawl on top of him, pink cheeked and giggling.

"So…we'll go see my dad tomorrow at the jail? Ask him about the money."

Ray let the daydream end as reality encroached. He wanted to go right now but he could see that Morgan was done in. And he knew that Lisa's bedtime varied only slightly on the weekends. And federal authorities were very strict about rules like visiting times for prisoners.

"Yeah. First thing."

Morgan looked scared all over again but there was no helping it.

"I have to put Lisa to bed."

He heard Lisa complain and the television snap off. Lisa slowed at his door and stared at him before her mother pushed her along. Lisa's room and his shared a wall and hers was at the end of the hallway. A few minutes later Lisa walked past his room again wearing pink pajamas that made her look about seven instead of ten. Who was that girl's father?

Had he died like Ray's or simply slipped away? He couldn't imagine having a child…or a woman like Morgan. They seemed so normal and unprepared for the chaos that had swept them up. Why would Karl do this? Money didn't seem like enough reason to leave these two to the wolves. He hoped like heck that Karl hadn't planned on abandoning them and taking the cash. It would be hard to keep his temper if that was the case. Ray had always been in loose control of his temper and there were many places to lose it. One place he had never lost his temper was with a woman or a child. Never had. Never would. Was that why Kenshaw had chosen him?

Ray checked his mail and texts. Lisa appeared in the door with her mother at her back.

"Good night, Mr. Strong. Thank you for saving my mom tonight."

Ray stood to face the child, feeling as out of place as a war club at a child's tea party. He shrugged by way of a reply.

"Mom says you were an army man."

Ray winced. "Marines."

"I'm glad you know how to fight. Do you have a little girl, too?"

Ray glanced at Morgan whose expression told her that Lisa had gone off script.

"No. I don't."

"A wife?"

"Not one of those either."

Lisa's smile seemed satisfied and her eyes glittered with devilment. Ray knew when he was being set up. Normally he'd be saying good-night, which he was, but this time he'd be staying under the same roof with Morgan right across the hall.

"I'll see you in the morning." Lisa strode forward and offered her hand.

Ray hesitated. She was thin and tiny and her hand was so very small. But he shook hers as if sealing some deal.

Then she surprised him again by thanking him formally in perfect Tonto Apache.

"My grandfather taught me that," she said.

He watched Lisa pad from the room on bare feet and wondered what else Karl had taught her.

THE NEXT MORNING Ray woke to the sound of a shovel rasping against gravel and earth. He headed for the window that faced the backyard. The sun wasn't even up and there was Guy Heron digging up the tire planter in the backyard. The ceramic toad lay on its side next him, one eye staring up at the sky. Ray swore and then tugged on his jeans.

He hoped the guy didn't have a job that required him to see out of both eyes.

Ray was out the door a moment later. The day was gray and the air temperature lower than crisp. Heron took another shovelful of earth and dumped it on the ceramic frog. Then he knelt to check inside the hole.

Ray's approach was soundless, not just because of his bare feet whispering over the ground but because of his training here on the reservation and with the US Marines. But still Heron spotted him before he reached him. The man sprang to his feet, gripped his shovel and ran across the driveway that separated the Hooke territory from the Herons', but there was no distinction as all land here was communal. There Heron stopped as if protected by some invisible boundary, the kind that Anglos drew all over the earth. He expected better from a member of his own tribe.

"I didn't find anything."

Ray kept coming. Heron made his second mistake of the day. He held his ground.

"This here is my property." He motioned with the shovel at a line that was not there and then lifted the shovel as if he intended to use it like an ax.

Third mistake, thought Ray as he came to a stop.

"This here?" he asked, marking the line that didn't exist with an index finger.

Heron nodded.

Ray did a fair impression of a mime meeting an invisible wall. Heron's brow knit as Ray seemed flummoxed by the barrier. His big finale was jabbing Heron in the eye.

Heron's knees buckled but Ray grabbed him by the collar before he fell to his face. Then he dragged him back across the driveway and to the hole he had been digging.

"You taking up horticulture?" asked Ray.

Heron struggled, choked and dropped his shovel.

Ray threw him onto the freshly dug soil.

"He just planted these," said Heron. "Right before the shooting."

Ray placed his fists on his hips and admired the speed with which Heron's eye swelled shut.

"Last night I told you that you should stay away from Morgan and her girl."

"And I didn't go near them."

Ray pointed at the ground. "This counts."

"I just thought, you know, maybe I could help her find it." He motioned toward the hole.

Ray grabbed Heron's wrist. A moment later he had that wrist behind Heron's back and the man's cheek pressed into the earth to the edge of the hole.

"Don't help her anymore because if you do, I'm going to use your shovel to bury you in this hole." He forcibly turned Heron's head so he got a mouthful of the dirt. "Do we understand each other?"

Heron spat and wiggled but stopped when Ray increased the pressure on his wrist and shoulder.

"All right!"

Ray held him a breath longer by pressing his knee in his back, using it to stand back up. Then he offered his hand to Heron who ignored it as he drew himself up, glared at Ray and moved toward his home in a gait that was as close as a man can come to a jog without jogging.

Ray followed him to the driveway, carrying the shovel Guy had abandoned in his haste. When Guy turned back, Ray sent his shovel after him. The man made a squeak of alarm and broke into a run. There was nothing like the satisfaction that comes from doing what you love, thought Ray.

When he turned toward the house, he saw the shocked faces of both Morgan and Lisa in the window of Lisa's bedroom. He dusted off his hands and headed toward the house. He tried not to let their looks of shock and horror affect him. He was doing what he'd been sent here to do, but frightening Lisa didn't sit well and Morgan now looked at him as if someone had let a wild animal loose in her home.

In fact that was exactly what had happened, but until someone found that money that was just the way it was going to be.

Chapter Eight

Morgan gasped as Ray pursued Guy to the driveway and tossed his shovel after her neighbor like a spear. The blade bit deep into the earth and the handle vibrated. Morgan blinked at the bunching muscles of Ray's back and the ease with which he tossed his captive aside.

He turned toward the house and his gaze flicked to hers. He stared at her and then stalked toward the kitchen door.

"Get dressed," Morgan ordered Lisa as she headed to the kitchen.

A moment later Ray was there, filling the room, and the sight of him, shirtless and glistening with sweat, was enough to make even the weakest heart pulse faster.

Earlier, while she'd been making coffee, she couldn't help reliving Ray's embrace. Just his arms about her caused lightning strikes of excitement to rip through her. She'd never felt anything like that. Not even with Larry, Lisa's father. She tried not to think of Larry but Lisa sometimes reminded her of him, affecting a mannerism she could not know her father had used. Morgan admitted she had been crazy in love with Larry, foolishly, wholeheartedly, but even when they had been intimate, her body had not churned and trembled as it did with Ray Strong, whom she barely knew. How was that even possible?

She wasn't the sort of woman who took chances, especially on a man as compelling and dangerous as Ray. But she wished she'd let him kiss her, just once. Just for herself. She knew that he was the complete opposite of the sort of guy she and Lisa needed. She needed safe, steady and solid. Ray was none of those things. But he was sexy as all get out. And the truth was that she was attracted to him.

"What are you doing?" she asked now, trying to stop the direction of her thoughts.

He explained what had happened.

"Dad's hummingbird garden?"

She managed to tear her gaze from all that naked male flesh and retreat to her bedroom for a view of the backyard. Sure enough, the bushes were lying on the ground.

"Why that…" She didn't say the word, but she thought it. She turned back to see Ray, now wearing an olive green T-shirt, thank goodness, filling the gap in the open door.

"He was looking for the money," he said.

Her mind flashed her a perfect image of Guy holding Lisa by the shoulders with that guilty look on his face. Morgan found her own fists clenching as the urge to protect her daughter ripped through her like a wave.

Ray glanced toward Lisa's room.

Lisa had told the Herons and that was enough to make the man she had known all her life dig up her dad's newly planted butterfly garden. She'd thought she knew her neighbor and it seemed she didn't know him at all. She felt adrift without the anchor of her father's presence and with the lost money making friends unrecognizable, she did not know who to trust. And poor Lisa had just lost her best friend because Morgan was not letting her visit the Herons any time soon. It was just devastating all around.

"He thought it was out there," she said. "I need to see Dad."

"Visiting hours are nine to three today. I checked."

"I should call ahead." Morgan noted that Ray was now staring at her freshly made bed. His gaze flashed to her next. He didn't say anything, just performed a military-style turn and disappeared down the hall.

With his disappearance, Morgan found she could breathe again. She checked on Lisa, already dressed, and quickly braided her hair as Lisa fired questions at her. Morgan left Lisa in the bathroom before returning to the kitchen to make a call to the corrections facility in Phoenix. It had taken over a month for her to get their names on the approved visitors list for her father. Now she told them she would be visiting and gave them her father's name. She'd learned that sometimes her dad was not available and once he had been moved temporarily before seeing the grand jury.

She had been prepared to hear he was unavailable, but when they told her why she would not be seeing him at the facility, she felt sick. Morgan pressed a hand on the counter for stability.

Ray set aside his coffee and moved to the opposite side of the counter. Morgan had gone pale and he knew something was very wrong.

"But why?" she asked.

Ray was beside her, clasping her elbow. She used her free hand to clutch his, her grip tight and her fingers cold.

"And the reason?… Yes." She nodded. "I can find it. May I see him?"

She listened, thanked the speaker and then disconnected. Her eyes were tearing up when she looked at him.

"He didn't tell me," she whispered.

"Tell you what?" asked Ray.

"The cancer. He said he was in remission. But it's back. It's been back but he never said. And it's really bad now. He's in the hospital." She sagged against him and he gathered her up, trying to feel guilty that Karl's illness had brought Morgan into his arms and failing.

"Shouldn't they have called you?" asked Ray.

"He told them not to. They said it was up to him."

Ray found himself in the unfamiliar position of organizing what needed to be done. Lisa would spend the day with Morgan's uncle, Agustin Tsosie, and his wife, Melouise. Ray called Kenshaw, who encouraged him to go visit Karl and report back on anything he might tell his daughter. He told Morgan to pack an overnight bag and any cash she had on hand.

Then he drove them to the hospital in Phoenix. On the drive, Morgan told him that her father had been diagnosed with prostate cancer. But he had been treated and had been in remission for six years. She had lost her mom, Adril, in a single-car accident with a deer. Lisa was only seven when she lost her grandmother.

Ray thought of his own accident, completely his fault, in Darabee when he'd been so drunk he'd totaled his car. Thank God he'd been the only one hurt. Living with a criminal record was preferable to causing injury or death to someone like Morgan's mom. He'd always felt stupid for his recklessness. Now he felt lucky. He hadn't killed anyone and he'd survived to learn something. Still, he wasn't proud of his behavior. He'd just been so angry.

It had been the day after they heard Hatch's body had finally been found and that he had likely died while being tortured in Iraq. He thought of his own parents' deaths. Was it better to have time to say goodbye or to be torn from this world without warning? Ray somehow thought that Morgan was lucky. At least she had time to tell her father goodbye.

What was a good death, anyway? He didn't know. But he knew a bad one. Hatch Yeager's death had been long and painful. Ray bore his part in that death on his soul.

They reached the hospital in Phoenix and were shown to her father's room to discover him recovering from surgery. He was unconscious and restrained, his wrist punctured with an IV and fixed to the metal bed rail with a thick plastic zip tie.

The nurse on duty suggested they step outside and explained that they had believed he was suffering from a gallstone until they went in and saw that the systemic cancer from his prostate had spread. Metastasized they had called it. Hospice care had been considered and rejected because her father was in his final days.

Morgan was a weeping mess when they went back into her father's room. She sobbed on her father and he did not rouse. The nurse came back in to check on him and said they had given him something for the pain.

Ray leaned against the window frame as Morgan settled in a vinyl chair at her father's side.

"I don't understand any of this," she said.

"Why he did what he did and why he never told us he was so ill." Morgan pressed a hand to her forehead. "I'd been after him because he was losing weight." She stroked her father's arm and Ray wondered if anyone would be there to sit with him as he passed from this world to the next.

The room was quiet except for the blip and beep of the machines monitoring Karl's IV and his heart. Karl had a strong heart, Ray knew, and a good one. But he'd miscalculated when it came to the payoff. Perhaps he had thought no one but Morgan would know. That he would have time to tell her where it was hidden.

"He took the job because he was dying," said Ray.

Morgan glanced back at him, the frown forming a line between her brows.

"He's the perfect choice. Dying and with a family to support."

"So you believe he was paid to shoot Sanchez and he did it for me and Lisa."

Ray nodded.

"Who paid him?"

That was what everyone wanted to know. Ray shrugged. A better question was who knew her father was so ill? That person might be the link between her father and whoever hired him. Ray thought a man like Karl might tell his army buddies or possibly his shaman. Ray decided to call Jack about that one.

"This makes no sense. Ovidio Sanchez was already in custody. He was going to prison, probably to get the death penalty, so why bother to kill him?"

Ray wondered how anyone could be so innocent and yet a mother. She ought to know something of how the world worked. Sometimes he wished he didn't.

"He was going to be interrogated by the FBI. They were there to take him into federal custody," said Ray.

Morgan blinked at him and he saw the moment she understood.

"The mine shooting. It wasn't a random act of violence. Was it?"

Ray shook his head.

"Sanchez was paid, too?"

"No evidence of that. But he was tied up with

some fanatical extremists. Survivalists and…"
Ray did not want her to know more than she had
to. "Crazy folks with crazy notions. Ones willing to use violence to make a point or get what
they want."

"But that mine. It was a giant hole in the
ground. Just a horrible scar on the earth. That
mining company should be ashamed, but what
did that shooting do besides take human lives?"

Ray knew from Jack that it had also eliminated
the man who had been stealing an unknown quantity of explosives from the mine and who had
been delivering them to the extremists in an outfit called BEAR. This was from Jack's brother,
Carter, whose wife, Amber, had noticed the thefts
and nearly died in the mass shooting as a result.

"That mass shooting wasn't random," Ray said.
"There were a lot of explosives stolen."

"I didn't hear that."

"You wouldn't. But that was why Sanchez
killed those folks. To shut them up. Your father
stopped the FBI from interrogating Sanchez."

Morgan shook her head. "No. He didn't do
that."

But Ray saw by the horror in her expression
that, despite her denial, she believed him.

Her hands covered her face and she wept. Ray
rubbed her back and stared down at her father,
dying in his hospital bed.

Morgan reined herself in and Ray thought it might be better if she had cried herself out. She now sat still and quiet with her thoughts. Ray left to buy them some sandwiches. Morgan didn't eat much. The doctor came in and gave her a dismal report on details that boiled down to the fact that the cancer was systemic. He did not offer an opinion of how long Karl had left.

Later, Morgan called her daughter to check on her and to report that "Pop-Pop" wasn't doing well. Lisa wanted to see him and Morgan said they'd try to arrange it.

Kenshaw Little Falcon arrived in the evening and he sat with her father so Ray could take Morgan down to the cafeteria for dinner. When they returned, her father was speaking to their shaman but Karl was only semiconscious and seemed to think he was back in Vietnam.

Ray watched his shaman with Karl and wondered if this was the man who had enlisted Morgan's dad for his deadly mission.

Kenshaw left at around ten and Morgan sat a vigil while Ray stretched out on the couch in the lounge. He checked on her in the night, seeing her still in the chair with her head on the bedding. She woke when the nurse came in to check on her dad. His heart rate was slow and his breathing even worse.

The doctor arrived around six to make rounds.

He asked Morgan to step out for a few minutes and said he would come find her in the lounge. He met them shortly thereafter and said he was uncertain if her father would wake again. His organs were shutting down.

There was a commotion in the hall and the doctor left them. Ray and Morgan discovered the staff rushing into and out of her father's room.

Ray knew before Morgan. They kept them out of the room but were unable to revive Karl. He had chosen the one moment he was alone to leave them, taking with him the answers that his daughter needed so desperately.

Chapter Nine

Ray took care of contacting Karl's pastor at the gospel church where he was a member. He spoke to the tribal council chairman who would send the necessary paperwork to get assistance for Karl's burial. He drove Morgan to the Phoenix detention center to pick up Karl's personal belongings from the deputy warden at the prison. They didn't amount to much. Just his wallet, an old phone, a few dollars, his medicine bundle and the turquoise ring and bracelet he always wore.

During the following four days, Morgan's house became a magnet for families bearing casseroles and friends of her father but far too many of them wanted to ask Morgan the same questions. Ray only had to physically toss out one persistent guy who did not have the manners his parents taught him.

He helped Morgan work with the funeral parlor to make arrangements for the viewing and funeral, which was scheduled for Friday afternoon.

Thursday night Morgan stopped him in the hall before he could escape to Karl's room. He was finding Morgan more and more distracting from his job here.

"I want to thank you for all you've done," she said, her delicate hand resting on his bare forearm. The contact made him twitch in all the wrong places.

"Well, that's why Kenshaw sent me."

"He sent you to protect me. But you've done so much more. The flowers, the casket, the funding through the tribe. I'm very grateful."

How grateful? he wanted to ask as his gaze fixed on her pink mouth. Instead he said, "It's nothing personal. I'm doing a job. When it's over, I'll be leaving." He met her gaze and held it. "You know that, right?"

Some of the gratitude left her and now he read worry or perhaps indecision there. *Be wise*, he wanted to say. But another part of him wanted to kiss her. She'd had Lisa with no husband. He'd learned that much from Jack. So she was not always wise and she was not always shy.

"I understand."

She didn't move away.

"Do you? Morgan, I'm a mistake. You know it and I know it."

Her fingers splayed over his bicep, lifting the tiny hairs on his forearm as she moved to stroke his bare skin. She lifted the sleeve of his gray T-shirt, pushing the fabric up and away to expose the tattoo there. The symbols had been chosen for him by his medicine man. Eagle Warrior, his shaman had called him. It was a spirit totem that could not have been further from Ray's personality. Perhaps that was why Kenshaw had chosen the eagle.

"What's this?" she asked.

"Kenshaw told me to get this when I joined the Turquoise Guardians."

"Your medicine society," she said. Her father had been a member. He wondered what she knew. "My father has something similar only his animal totem is the puma. I did not know it was related to the Turquoise Guardians."

His brows lifted. A lion was a powerful totem, a clever dangerous hunter. Karl had been all that.

She traced the outline of the medicine shield branded in colorful ink upon his upper arm, pausing at the turquoise and the cross that appeared tied to the outer hoop.

"He doesn't have this."

Morgan's fingers grazed over the five feathers hanging from the hoop and reaching nearly to the junction of his elbow.

"Five," she said as she stroked the final feather.

Ray winced at the pain that cramped his insides.

They had added, one for each of them, the inductees, the best friends, but only four had returned from Iraq. Hatch had come home later in a box draped in an American flag.

"Why an eagle?" she asked, referring to the image in the center, the crying head of a bald eagle in profile, it's yellow eye and yellow beak both bright and sharp.

"Eagles have good sight. They can see things a long way off," said Ray. And Kenshaw said that Ray needed help with that, needed to see things before they happened. Needed to have better judgment. Like now, for instance, when the heat of her body clouded his thoughts.

He told her then about the feathers, one for Jack and Carter and Dylan and him and Hatch. He watched her brows crease at the mention of Hatch Yeager. This reservation was too small for her not to know that Hatch had been reported MIA and then, four years later, his body had come home to be buried in the tribe's cemetery. Did she know he had been held captive for years before they killed him and dumped him in the desert?

He wasn't sure. But he knew Morgan understood loss. Her mother, now her father and before that a brother. Ray heard about that, of course, even in Iraq—such news traveled fast.

"I remember Hatch," she said. "You two were best friends."

"Yes."

She traced the final feather again. It was the only one turned backward. "You must miss him terribly."

He didn't talk about Hatch. Not even with the men who were there that night. Especially not with them, though they all carried the visible tribute to his memory drawn in ink upon their bodies. But he found himself talking again. Morgan did not interrupt. She just stood there in her skimpy tank top and the flannel shorts she slept in with one hand pressed over his heart while Ray spoke in words that came slowly at first. He explained about how the perimeter needed to keep insurgents from attacking their convoys. The two Humvees and how he had tricked his way in by adding his name to their commanding officer's orders before he finished. He never expected SFC Mullins to actually let him ride in that first Humvee. Everyone knew that Mullins preferred Hatch because he was easygoing and followed orders. But Ray had gotten away with it, sending Hatch into the second vehicle with Tromgartner, who had an annoying a habit of clicking his tongue incessantly on the roof of his mouth. Hatch had grinned at him, knowing what Ray had pulled, as he climbed into the second Humvee with Tromgartner, Carter Bear Den and their translator.

"It drove Hatch crazy," said Ray. The memory made him feel physically sick. If not for that joke, it would have been his body flying through space, landing on the hill too far away to reach before the insurgents got him.

"And so he was in the truck that got ambushed?" asked Morgan.

"It was an insurgent attack. The second Humvee was closer to the enemy position. They threw explosives. Two of our men were captured. One was killed."

"The lucky one," she said.

How did she understand that?

"Yes."

"Have people told you this wasn't your fault?" she asked.

He gritted his teeth and nodded.

"It doesn't help, though, does it?"

He met her gaze and couldn't believe what she had said. No one ever said that.

"Not at all."

"Everyone said things to me after my brother's suicide. Instead of helping, it made me so angry."

That was exactly how he felt, too.

Ray looked away before replying. "They mostly said things about the nature of war, like they had been through one or about fate. But that's not true.

I'm here and Hatch is dead because my sergeant clicked his tongue and because I let Hatch endure it rather than suffer myself."

She didn't say the next most obvious thing—that he hadn't known. Couldn't have known what that one small action would reap. Because that didn't help either. It just made him angry all over again. He lifted his gaze and waited for her to speak. When she did, she surprised him again.

"That must be a heavy load to bear." She slid her hand away.

She understood him because she'd had to deal with the aftermath of her brother's suicide. But her younger brother had been four years behind Morgan and five behind him, so Ray had been in the service when he had jumped. Ray didn't know him. Now he never would.

How many nights had she lain awake wondering if she could have stopped him? Now she had lost her dad, too.

"How do you bear it?" he asked.

"Some days are worse than others. I spend a lot of time thinking how old Mateo would be now and what he might be doing."

Ray now found himself in the uncomfortable position of wanting to express his sympathy but not say something predictable.

"I wish I had known him."

That made her smile. "Me, too. Come on. I have beer in the refrigerator."

They sat at the kitchen counter and drank the one can of beer in two small glasses sitting side by side.

Morgan picked up the conversation. "My biggest mistake was trusting Lisa's father, which is a lot easier to bear than yours. And as it turned out, it was the luckiest bad luck I ever had. Like you, I never talk about it."

"You don't have to," he said.

"I know that."

Ray studied his nearly empty glass and swirled the foam that clung to the bottom. She had listened to him. He should do the same. But he found he wanted to slip out the back door instead. Morgan's secrets were none of his business.

"Is it the secret you are wary of or the intimacy?" she asked.

He sipped his beer. "Both," he admitted.

"I was seventeen when I met Lisa's father. He was handsome, employed and madly in love with me. I was young, foolish and mistook infatuation for love. He was very good to me and made promises. He even gave me a ring." She held out her bare left hand as if to show him the ring that had once circled her slim finger.

Had he broken it off or had she?

"When I told him I was pregnant, things changed.

He grew restless and preoccupied. Then he disappeared. I was worried. It was so unlike him and it reminded me of the time before they found Mateo.

"But he wasn't missing." Her laugh was harsh and her flush showed embarrassment. "I even reported it to the police." She shifted to face him. "Do you know what they told me?"

He didn't.

"No such person. He didn't exist. So whose child was this?" She laid a hand on her flat stomach. "I found him in one of the places we used to meet. He was with another young woman, dark like me. Mexican, I think."

"Did you bust his nose?" ask Ray.

"No, I followed him home. He lives in Darabee, works for the city sanitation department and has a wife and three young children."

Ray slapped an open hand on the counter so hard the glasses jumped. Then he used some language he'd learned in the sandbox. Morgan smiled.

"Yeah, exactly. I came back home to my parents and told them everything. They helped me raise Lisa. She's turned out to be the best thing in my life. So I'm not sorry. Just ashamed at how naive I was back then."

"You could have him arrested."

"No. It's too long ago. Statute of limitation is

up. And I'd rather raise her alone than have her anywhere near him."

"Child support?"

"Not worth the risk."

Ray nodded. "Would you like me to…"

She shook her head.

"I can be discreet. He wouldn't know."

"Ray, you are my protector. Not my avenger."

He looked down at the swallow of beer at the bottom of the juice glass, really wanting to punch that guy.

"You know eagles don't just look down to see what others cannot," said Morgan. "They also fly higher than any other living thing. They carry our messages to the creator and they are holy. Deeply sacred. Perhaps your shaman wanted you to remember that you are also blessed."

"Or to carry his messages for him," said Ray.

"I don't think so. He wants you to see yourself as other see you."

"As a badass? Screw-up? Poster boy for regret?"

"Look around, Ray. Not backward. That's not where we live. We live here now. In this time and place."

Live in the moment. See what was all around him. Ray settled back on the kitchen stool and pushed away his glass.

"You better get to bed. Funeral tomorrow."

He rose. She touched his cheek and he let his

eyes slide closed for a moment as he considered pursuing what she seemed to be offering. Then he flicked his gaze to hers. She was not looking for a one-nighter, and she sure didn't deserve a guy dragging an entire boatload of baggage. She was making a connection and instead of welcoming it, he was shutting it down because he already liked her too much to be her next mistake.

"We do live in this moment," he said. "And you are right. I spend too much time in the past. But you have a daughter, Morgan. That means you must look forward to a future that won't include me."

Her hand dropped and she let him go. It was hard to walk away because he knew she was the best woman he'd ever known. But she was a mother, not a plaything. And he had no idea how to be a husband or father. You didn't need eagle vision to see that.

THE FUNERAL WAS better attended than it should have been, considering Karl's recent actions. But there were friends and members of his clan, his tribe and the VFW—Veterans of Foreign Wars—not to mention an unfortunate number of curiosity seekers from Darabee and the surrounding area. It was hard to know how to celebrate Karl's life. He had been a basket man. In the long-ago time, weaving baskets was a man's work while the women typically made the pottery. There were few left—male or female—who wove baskets like Karl. He was a veteran of the Vietnam War, a father and grandfather, a brother and son. He was also a paid assassin.

Ray wondered how many attendees sought clues to finding the missing two hundred thousand. That kind of money had a long tail. Ray had organized the funeral, his first, with the help of the family's pastor and Kenshaw Little Falcon. No one wanted to speak or sing, so Ray asked the other two remaining members of Tribal Thunder to make a drum circle and sing some of the old songs as they had done before joining the US Marines. He missed Carter Bear Den but not half as much as Jack did. Dylan Tehauno was in fine voice and offered his help to watch over Morgan in the days to come.

That was the kind of friendship money couldn't buy.

After the funeral, neighbors and family gathered at Morgan's house. They ate much of the food they had brought and stayed too long. Guy Heron had arrived with his wife and two girls. Lisa and Ami had disappeared into the bedroom with the cat. Guy remained on the opposite side of the room from Ray and no matter where Ray moved, Guy moved in opposition. Morgan sat in a dining room chair now in the living room with her uncle Agustin Tsosie as Agustin's second wife, Melouise, wrapped up leftovers and put them away.

Lisa returned from the bedrooms with Ami trailing behind. Lisa was carrying the bag that had come from the deputy warden and held it out to her mother.

"What's this, Mama?"

Morgan turned to Lisa and looked at the bracelet she held. The sterling silver had a nice patina and the large center piece of turquoise was made more stunning by the black spider web pattern and bright sky blue color.

"That's your Pop-Pop's bracelet, Lisa. You know that."

"No. What's this?" Lisa pointed to the inside of the bracelet.

Ray moved closer and so did Mr. Heron. Morgan's uncle leaned forward.

"It's a maker's mark," said Morgan.

"Next to that. These scratches," said Lisa and pointed.

Heron now stretched his neck to see, spotted Ray watching him and stepped back.

Morgan sensed the audience and took the bracelet. "You shouldn't be in your grandfather's room or touching his things. Put it back."

Lisa did and all eyes followed her as she made her way down the hall and out of sight.

A piece like that had once been the only form of collateral accepted for loans to their people. Loans made in trading posts via pawning the silver jewelry. So, it was called old pawn. It seemed this piece had come to Karl through his family and Lisa knew it well enough to spot something new. And if what Lisa said was accurate, then this would bring more trouble. It didn't take very long.

Ray watched Guy excuse himself to use the bathroom. Ray asked Jack and Dylan to watch Morgan as he headed after him. When Guy left the bathroom and turned the wrong way he was surprised to find Ray already in Karl's room.

"Looking for something?" asked Ray.

Guy said nothing as he reversed course.

Ray remained in the bedroom and was disappointed to see Morgan's uncle also make his way in there. Two men left the gathering by the front door but detoured past Karl's window and peered inside. It was well past dark when Jack returned to tell him that the last of the guests had left the grounds.

But Ray knew that some of them would be back.

Chapter Ten

"Do you know why Amber is in protective custody?" Kenshaw Little Falcon asked as Ray walked him to his car.

"She's a witness to the mass shooting," said Ray.

"Shooter is dead."

And she and Carter had not left protective custody. As far as Ray knew, not even his twin brother, Jack, knew where they were.

"Amber still has to testify against that crazy brother of the dead cop from Darabee, Orson Casey."

"Yes. But also she overheard a man's name down in Lilac. That's all. She was just standing in the hallway outside her boss's door and heard him speak a name into his telephone. Now her supervisor is dead and that man, that very dangerous man, wants her to disappear just like Ovidio Sanchez."

"What name?" asked Ray.

"Theron Wrangler. He's a documentary film-maker out of Phoenix."

"That doesn't sound dangerous."

"He is also an activist."

"Like me?" Ray thumbed his chest and then extended a finger in Kenshaw's direction. "Or you?"

"More like me. He's a founding member of PAN."

Protect All Nature. Ray had been a member, too, at one time, back before Iraq and Hatch's capture. Back when he thought he could make a difference.

Kenshaw told Ray that the FBI were now watching Wrangler and searching for any clues that could lead them to the explosives.

"You think Karl knew this?"

"Karl told me they spoke to him. He wouldn't tell me anything more."

"But you put his name in the hat. Right?"

Kenshaw stared up at the glittering stars. When he spoke, it seemed as if he spoke to the wind.

"I didn't know what the job was until afterward. Just that it paid well and they wanted a man who would not pose a risk like Sanchez."

"A suicide mission," Ray clarified.

"A chance to serve the cause. I didn't know they selected him or that he'd agreed until after his arrest."

Ray had a sour taste in his mouth.

Kenshaw still stared at the heavens. "He wouldn't tell me who hired him or what he had done with the money. Karl said they didn't tell him why they wanted Sanchez killed although he assumed that they wanted Sanchez silenced before he could speak to the FBI. Whatever Sanchez knew, it threatened someone and Karl took that information to his grave. I don't know who hired Karl."

"But you know who you spoke to when you suggested him."

"I do."

"You have to tell that to our tribal police."

"I do not have to."

"The FBI. They need to stop them before they use those explosives."

Kenshaw heaved a heavy breath.

"You are supposed to protect our tribe."

"That is what I am doing. You keep Morgan safe. That's all you must do."

Ray suddenly did not know who was really giving him orders. Was it his spiritual leader or a man who worked with terrorists?

"Did Karl speak of this when you visited at the hospital?" asked Kenshaw.

"He was unconscious, so he didn't say anything."

"You were with Morgan the entire night?"

"No, but…" He didn't like the way Kenshaw was looking at him. "She doesn't know anything."

"You can't be certain. He was awake when I got there."

"And he thought he was in Hanoi."

"Yet he asked me again to look after his girls."

Ray glowered at Kenshaw. Jack had expressed his doubts to him already. Was their shaman looking out for Morgan or just himself?

"You need to find out what she knows," said Kenshaw.

"Why?"

"Because if you don't, some very bad men are going to consider Morgan a threat. If that happens even you won't be able to protect her."

But damned if he wouldn't try. This time he was not going to mess up.

"I could turn you in," said Ray.

"Yes and that would cause immediate concern to these men."

Stalemate, Ray realized.

"If we can't convince them that Morgan is in the dark, then I'll have to pull you. I don't want you to die with her."

"No one is dying. You sent me to protect her and that's what I'll do."

"The best way to protect her is to find that money and find out if she knows who hired her father."

A shiny black Escalade with tinted windows

pulled up in the street before Morgan's modest home, looking as out of place, in a neighborhood of used cars and late-model pickups, as an alien spacecraft.

"Feds," said Kenshaw. "Stay with her during questioning if you can."

"What if they try to take her?" asked Ray, already bracing for a fight.

"Can't. She's on sovereign land and has committed no crime. They can't even be here without tribal council escort."

As if cued by Kenshaw's words, a silver SUV pulled in behind the FBI. On the side of the vehicle was written: Tribal Police Chief. The driver exited first. Out stepped their police chief, Wallace Tinnin, who paused to retrieve his cowboy hat. The opposite door slammed and tribal council member Zach Gill appeared rounding the hood.

"And there they are," said Ray.

"Tinnin is a fair man. Can't see anyone better to have with her." He gave Ray a long look. "Except you."

Kenshaw had a lot of faith in him. Too much, Ray thought.

MORGAN HAD NEVER even seen a real FBI agent— let alone one that was Apache. But here he stood in her kitchen amid the many dishes neatly covered in plastic wrap. Field agent Luke Forrest introduced himself as Black Mountain Apache. He was tall and lean with short black hair sprinkled with a few gray hairs at the temples. His hollow cheeks showed he did not eat enough, but his wide shoulders spoke of power contained in a tailored gray suit. With him was field agent Cassidy Cosen. She was his opposite, short, blonde and fair. They shared a serious expression along with the matching badges and pistols clipped to their belts.

Cassidy took a long look at field agent Cosen. She had taken the name of her husband, a tribal council member of the Black Mountain Apache tribe. This woman Morgan had heard of because she had a friend on Black Mountain who told her of the Anglo who adopted an Apache girl, thinking she was Brule Sioux. She was now married to the brother of the child she adopted. It was like having a celebrity right here in her home.

She offered coffee and one of the many plates of cookies but the agents declined. They didn't look the type for cookies, she realized.

"We are sorry to have to disturb you so late," said Forrest. He had a military bearing and was slender, cutting a fine figure in his Anglo suit. The shiny gold badge flashed as he placed a hand on his trim hip.

"And on the day she has buried her father," said Ray, his voice a growl.

Councilman Gill was a gentleman, and he and Chief Tinnin both accepted a mug of coffee.

Agent Cosen did not observe the custom of speaking some pleasantries as a prelude to the purpose of their visit. He went right to the heart of the matter with the precision of a diving hawk.

"We now believe your father was paid to kill Ovidio Sanchez. We know your father cashed a bank check for two hundred thousand dollars. Are you currently in possession of this money?"

Morgan looked from the fierce blonde woman to Ray who gave the slightest incline of his head.

"I am not," said Morgan.

The questions continued with the FBI obviously not receiving the answers they would have liked. Did they expect her to reach into a casserole dish and pull out wads of cash? She didn't have it and didn't know anything about it except what she had heard from the bank manager. Agent Forrest relayed that the bank manager was now in federal custody. If she did have it she wouldn't keep it. That was blood money and it tainted all it touched. But she had a sinking feeling that until the money was found, she and her daughter were in danger. Where could her father have hidden it? Her mind trailed to the days before the shooting. His disappearance in his truck. She was sure he'd used that time to stash the cash somewhere. But where?

"Tell him about Guy Heron," said Ray.

She did and about the many guests at the funeral that she did not know.

Forrest rubbed his jaw, thinking. Then he spoke to Ray.

"Your friend Carter Bear Den saw Sanchez down in Bisbee right after he left the mine. And his new wife, Amber Kitcheyan Bear Den, overheard her employer mention a man just after she reported an overage in a delivery."

An overage? Was that what the FBI called missing explosives now?

Her supervisor attempted to make a phone call to a certain party.

"Theron Wrangler," said Ray.

Forrest's brows shot upward.

"Carter told his brother who told me."

"Your medicine society," said Forrest. "I understand Morgan's father was also a member."

Kenshaw took that one. "Our society is a religious and cultural organization. We have no affiliation with eco-extremists."

"But you do," said Forrest to Kenshaw. "You protested in Sedona in the 1990s with PAN and were a known associate of Walter Fields, now in a federal detention center for acts of terrorism."

"We were protesting misuse of tribal water rights."

"Yes," said Forrest. "I am aware. But you were and are a member of PAN. And Fields is believed to have headed the eco-extremist group known as WOLF."

Kenshaw's mouth clamped shut.

"That's not an extremist group," said Ray. "They have members all over the country."

"Yes. I have one of their wall calendars, too. Has a buffalo for April this year. But here is the trouble. That Jeep tour outfit in Sedona that went up in flames two years ago, Crimson Excursions? Their fuel tanks caught because they were rigged with explosives. The residue left at the scene in Sedona from the explosion—the same explosion that resulted in the death of the owner, Warren Cushing—is a match for the ones taken from the mine in Lilac. Seems WOLF has moved up from selling calendars."

"But that happened two years ago," said Morgan.

"Exactly. Which means it was not arson, as reported to the public. We knew at the time that mining-grade explosives were used. Now we know the source and we know that the eco-extremist group claiming responsibility has been stealing explosives for at least two years prior to the mass-shooting at the Lilac Mine. It also means that we have no idea how much material they currently have in their possession or what they intend to use it for."

The implications settled over Morgan like a wet

wool blanket. She had to remind herself to breathe and when she did it came as a gasp.

"WOLF does not condone the taking of human life," said Kenshaw.

"But BEAR does," said Agent Cosen. "They not only condone it, they encourage it. Exterminate the species that threatens the planet—us."

"Your father was hired by WOLF or BEAR," said Forrest to Morgan.

"I don't know what that is," she said, shaking her head in dismissal even as the implication bit into her bones.

"WOLF is *Warriors of Land Forever*. They like to destroy property that infringes on natural places. Then there's BEAR. That stands for *Bringing Earth Apocalyptic Restoration*. Now these guys, they mean to end us. Bring the earth back to what they see as the natural order by any means possible. In other words they make no attempt to preserve human life."

"Why don't you shut them down?"

"Have to find them first," said Forrest. His gaze went to Kenshaw and held.

Morgan watched the unfolding drama. How had she ever gotten tangled up in all this?

Councilman Gill blew away a heavy breath and straightened. Everyone turned to give him their attention.

"Although we are alarmed to hear of the missing explosives, our prime concern is our tribe. I fear that stories of this money will cause a rush of treasure hunters onto our sovereign land."

That was already happening.

"I would remind you, Ms. Hooke," said the Anglo agent, "that it is illegal for you to keep any of the money tendered to your father for the purpose of murder for hire."

Morgan met her pale blue eyes, glassy and cold.

"I understand."

"Withholding evidence of a crime is also a violation of federal law," said Agent Cosen.

"I am not withholding anything. I didn't know what my father was going to do and I don't have the money."

It was clear from the hardening of the woman's mouth that she did not believe a word.

Chief Tinnin stood and thanked Morgan for the coffee, signaling an end to the meeting. He ushered the federal agents out and paused to say goodbye to Morgan in Tonto Apache. Then he turned to Ray.

"Find it quick," he said and then he was gone.

Just how were they supposed to do that?

Chapter Eleven

When Ray returned from speaking to Kenshaw it was to a quiet house. That made his heart jump as he called out.

"Morgan!"

She answered and Ray could breathe again.

He found Morgan on the bed in her father's room beside Lisa. Ray leaned against the door frame, watching them. The cat sauntered past him, flicking her tail against his leg before jumping up on the coverlet. Cookie then curled at the girl's side but the feline kept both ghostly green eyes on Ray.

"That's the last of them," he said.

Morgan nodded to Lisa who went to the closet and retrieved the small bag of her grandfather's effects. Lisa drew out the bracelet and handed it to her mother. Her father wore this bracelet every day and removed the ornament only when he slept. Yet suddenly it seemed a foreign object, out of place without him here to wear it. The grief made her throat ache and her hand began to tremble.

"Look inside," said Lisa.

He went to the window and closed the blind then came to stand at the foot of the bed.

Morgan borrowed her father's reading glasses from the bedside table where he had set them the morning he'd left and never come back. She had brought them with his medications, to the prison, but officials would not let him have the glasses because of the broken frame but did supply him with a free pair from the canteen. His glasses magnified the marks Lisa had found.

"It looks like a stick-figure man holding a medicine wheel," said Morgan.

A medicine wheel was a hoop, divided into four sections. Each section had multiple meanings. The first one, yellow, also meant east, youth and spring and the break of day, among other things. Morgan looked at the second figure. "This looks like a rabbit."

Ray looked next. There were two figures. One human. One animal. He could determine nothing else.

He handed the glasses and jewelry to Lisa who held the bracelet in one hand and the glasses like a magnifying glass in the other as she studied the scratches in the silver on the inside of the cuff bracelet. The entire image was only a half-inch high.

"Were they there before?" he asked Morgan.

"I'm not sure. I've never noticed them, but now I can't remember if I've ever seen the inside of this bracelet."

Lisa lifted her head. "I have. These are new."

Ray held Morgan's gaze and a chill made her shudder. She could tell he saw the danger in this and was assessing the risk.

"He knew it would come back to us," Morgan whispered.

Ray nodded.

Lisa continued to study the inside of the cuff. "This can't be a medicine wheel. It's not divided. And rabbits don't have long legs like that. The circle has a little dash inside and some dots at the bottom."

Morse code? wondered Ray.

Lisa stiffened and the hand holding the bracelet dropped to her lap.

"What?" asked her mother.

"I know what this is." Lisa's eyes twinkled as she looked from her mother to Ray and then back to her mother. "Pop-Pop made it for me! Don't you remember? When I was really little. He was sick and he was in that place."

"The clinic?"

"And he had to sit so long with the…" She tapped the junction of her elbow.

"The chemotherapy."

"And his hair fell out and came back white. He couldn't weave his baskets."

"He said it was too tiring," said Morgan, thinking back. Her daughter had been only four but she seemed to remember more than Morgan did.

"When he came home he started painting with those little brushes."

Morgan thought back, remembering the card table and the paints and brushes.

"Ceramics. He took a class at the community center."

Lisa set aside the bracelet and glasses and sprang to her feet. Then she ran to her room with Morgan and Ray in pursuit. From her bedside table, she lifted a six-inch ceramic statue of a gray-bearded prospector standing with an arm across the back of his mule. She passed the figurine to her mother.

In one of the prospector's hands was a circular gold pan painted the same leaden color as his beard. In the pan were tiny flecks of gold paint to represent specks of precious metal. Also in the gray pan was a solid rectangular area painted yellow with some tiny characters painted within that.

Morgan stepped forward, her brows knit. "That wasn't there before."

"What?" Lisa leaned over as her mother pointed to the yellow rectangle. "Get the glasses."

"I can read it," said Lisa, peering at the gold pan. "It says 12311989."

Morgan straightened and nearly dropped the statue.

"What does it mean?"

"It's a treasure hunt," said Ray, studying her. "And your mama understands the first clue."

RAY EASED THE statue back onto Lisa's nightstand. "He knew you'd receive his bracelet with his effects. And, failing that, he knew that Lisa would eventually notice the addition to her statue."

"But what does that mean," said Lisa. "It's just a bunch of numbers."

"It's my birthday," said Morgan. "December thirty-first, 1989."

"But that's not a clue," said Lisa.

Morgan's eyes rounded. "Lisa, you can't tell anyone at school about this."

"Mom, there is no school tomorrow. It's Saturday."

"You can't phone or text or chat. Nothing."

Lisa rolled her eyes. "Fine."

Ray dropped to a knee and took hold of Lisa's shoulders. "Lisa, there are a lot of people after your Pop-Pop's money. If they have this clue, they might hurt your mom to get her to tell them what it means."

Lisa's eyes grew wide. Morgan tugged at his hand.

"You're frightening her."

"She should be frightened. She told Guy Heron about the money and he dug up the backyard. Then tonight, right after Lisa brought out this bracelet, he tried to sneak into your dad's room."

Morgan sank to the bed. "Everyone at the house saw the bracelet."

"And heard her ask what the marks meant before you told her to put it away."

"Oh, no."

Lisa tucked in close to her mom. "Mama, did I do something wrong again?"

Morgan wrapped an arm about her daughter's narrow shoulders. "You have to listen to Mr. Strong. He's here to protect us."

Lisa lifted her head to stare at him, her eyes seeming to judge his strength and his will.

"What do we do?"

"RIGHT NOW WE get some sleep," said Morgan to Lisa. "Tomorrow can take care of itself."

Lisa did not rise from her grandfather's bed.

"What do I always tell you?" asked Morgan.

"We live in this moment. Everything else is illusion," Lisa recited by rote, but Morgan could see her heart wasn't in it.

Morgan rose and offered a hand, seeing Lisa out and to her bedroom to change for sleep. The cat followed Lisa like a duckling after its mother. Once Lisa was tucked in, Morgan did what she could to assure her daughter that everything would be fine, trying not to let Lisa see the real fear she had about their safety. She understood now why her shaman had sent Ray to them and she thanked God for it.

When she left Lisa's room, she found Ray in the hall. He had changed into the snug white muscle shirt he preferred for sleeping and the gray sweatpants that hugged his magnificent backside. Morgan cleared her throat but her heart continued to accelerate. It was difficult to be faced with so much temptation. She knew that he was here on an assignment and that he would leave when the trouble did. But she also knew how good he smelled, with his hair wet from a shower and his skin damp.

Morgan looked up at Ray standing watchful as an eagle, his arms folded.

Here was the only person she had told about her daughter's father and he had not been shocked or judgmental. But he had warned her off when, in a moment of weakness, she had really considered sleeping with him. She was considering it again and only her daughter sleeping in the room behind her kept her from offering herself. This was so bad. She wasn't that kind of woman. But it had been so long and she was attracted to Ray, not just because of how he looked, but because they had both suffered losses, made mistakes. He wasn't a bad man. He was all that stood between her and the bad men. She knew he was dangerous but not to her and not to Lisa.

It was only her need for his protection and her weeping heart that made her feel this desire to experience his hands on her body. She had just buried her father. It was normal for her emotions to be erratic.

"She asleep?" he asked.

"Nearly. It was a hard day."

Morgan stepped toward her bedroom and paused. It had been so long since she had been with a man. Ray wasn't perfect. But he was honest and he was a strange blend of vulnerability and toughness she found irresistible. But she needed to be wise, didn't she? She knew he would not be staying. What she didn't know was if that was a reason to resist her desires or one that meant she should act on them now before it was too late.

"I want Lisa to go to your uncle Agustin's tomorrow. I'm sending Dylan Tehauno along to keep watch over her."

Fear washed away the temptation as she met his serious expression with one of his own.

"We need to find that money and turn it over to the FBI."

"Will that stop all this?"

"We could just give them the clues and let them figure it out," she said.

"Yes, but they won't mean anything to them. They wouldn't have known what that symbol meant. And your birthday—that won't help them find the money. But I have a feeling you know what that number signifies and where to look next."

"I do."

"Then tomorrow we get Lisa somewhere safe and then we try to find this money."

She nodded. "Do you want some coffee?"

It was too late for coffee, but she wasn't ready to face her empty bed just yet. It never felt so lonely before Ray moved in. Whether because of her father's company or because she was busy raising Lisa and with work, Morgan had never really wanted a man in her life—until now. Now the nights were long and sleepless as she fought the urge to slip across the hall in the darkness.

"Water." He followed her down the hall to the kitchen.

The living room was suddenly illuminated with red and blue lights that spun around the walls.

"What's that?" she asked, moving to the living room to peer out the front door.

"Detective Bear Den set up a patrolman in front of your house."

He moved to stand behind her. His breath brushed her neck, lifting the hairs. She wanted to drop her head back against his chest, close her eyes and feel his body against hers. Instead she leaned forward to watch a tribal police officer emerge from his patrol car, flashlight in hand as he approached a dark pickup he had pulled over before her house. This housing development was on a loop that led in a half circle back to the road. The only reason to be on it was to get to one of seven houses.

The officer spoke with the driver and then the truck pulled out. The officer returned toward his unit and Ray slipped past her and out the door. She heard him ask and the officer answer. They were not from the tribe, but were Anglos. There was no need to ask what they wanted.

Ray stepped back inside. Morgan had her arms about herself because she couldn't seem to stop shivering. He took one look at her and drew her in, his arms rubbing up and down her back. She started crying of course. After today she was surprised she had any tears left to cry.

He ushered her to the sofa and they sat side by side.

"We have to find it. Make it stop," she said, and she looked up at his handsome face, seeing an expression of yearning mirroring her own.

Her hand slipped around his neck and she pressed her lips to his. He kissed her with a sweetness that defied everything she knew of his reputation. This kiss was full of comfort and tenderness. His hands were gentle as they gathered her in and rocked slowly with her. He kissed her cheeks and her neck and then he whispered in her ear.

"I'll keep you safe, Morgan. I swear on my life that nothing will happen to either you or Lisa."

She believed him. And suddenly she knew why their shaman had chosen him. It wasn't because he was a warrior or a former US Marine or a member of Tribal Thunder. It was because of Hatch Yeager, the friend he could not save. Kenshaw must have known that Ray would do anything to keep from losing another person he had sworn to protect. Morgan felt a terrible weight of responsibility pressing down on her. She needed to stay safe in order to protect Ray because she was certain he would dive on a grenade to protect her and her daughter. And she also knew that she could not live with that.

He stroked her hair and pressed her head against his chest so she could hear the steady thumping of his strong heart. She splayed a hand across his chest, trying to absorb just a little of that power, for she felt sure she would need it.

Ray took hold of her shoulders and eased her away.

"I have to ask you about your dad."

"All right."

"That day you took your father to Darabee, what do you remember?"

She thought back to that day in February and relayed what she recalled. The drive to the shopping area. Parking in the strip mall. Her dad telling her to meet him in forty-five minutes at a restaurant. Errands and her return to pick him up.

"Did he say who he was meeting?"

"No."

"Why he was meeting this person?"

"He just said he'd arranged to meet an old friend. A vet from his unit."

Ray made a face.

"That was a lie. Wasn't it?"

"Probably." He raked his long fingers through his thick hair. "Where did you go?"

"Grocery shopping. It's right across the highway from that restaurant."

"Was he waiting outside for you?"

"No, I came in and he was alone at a table near the windows."

"See anyone you knew?"

She thought. "I don't believe so."

"Think, Morgan."

She did. "Just some customers. Someone held the door for me." His face had been familiar but she couldn't place him. Where had she seen him before? "I saw the woman behind the counter and another filling the coffee carafes. It wasn't very busy. After breakfast and before lunch. There was a young mother with two kids. I asked their ages. But I didn't know her."

Ray did not seem relieved. This was important, but she really could not come up with a single name.

"I didn't know any of them."

His mouth twitched in what might have been an attempt at a smile.

"Okay. Fine," he said. "What then?"

"He asked me to drive him to the bank. I ran to the drugstore for a few personal items. When I came back he was already waiting in the car."

"Couldn't you get those things at the grocery store?"

"They're less expensive in the drugstore and I had a coupon."

He nodded.

The bank, she thought. "That was the money wasn't?"

"Did he have a bag or case?"

She shook her head.

"Two hundred thousand would take up some

space, so I don't think so. Unless he had it already hidden in your car."

She pressed a hand to her forehead.

"This is unreal."

Ray kept going, not giving her a minute to think.

"Now what about at the hospital, when I left to get us some food. Did your dad wake up?"

She shook her head.

"Did he say anything to you?"

"He was unconscious until our shaman arrived and then, well, you heard. It was just babbling."

Ray blew out a long breath. His shoulders relaxed. "All right. So the number, the one on the statue your dad gave Lisa."

He was clever and she wondered for just an instant if Kenshaw had sent him to find the money, which would make him just like everyone else. A part of her wanted to believe it because it was preferable to the alternative. That she had feelings for her protector that went beyond longing and gratitude. Was it better to be taken advantage of or to harbor foolish thoughts of a future with a man who had told her bluntly that this was a job to him?

Ray cleared his throat. "Why paint your birthday on a yellow rectangle in the middle of that gold pan?"

"It's not just a rectangle. Didn't you see the black circle before the numbers?"

He nodded, clearly not making the connection. Perhaps he had been right when he told her that her father had intended the message only for her.

Morgan hesitated. She knew exactly what that symbol meant and she knew where they needed to go next. The only question was whether to tell Ray or try to get to follow her father's clues alone.

She looked at the man who still held her in his arms. Could she trust him with what she knew?

Chapter Twelve

"Do you own cattle, Ray?" asked Morgan. She made her decision. For better or worse, she would trust the man her shaman had sent her.

Many of their tribe did. Some had been given land to ranch by the tribe, but most kept their cattle in the tribe's communal herd overseen by the tribal livestock manager.

Ray massaged the muscles at his left shoulder with his left hand as if suddenly developing a crick in his neck.

"Not anymore."

But he had. Most folks kept their cattle like money in the bank as insurance against a rainy day. She gave him a curious look.

He glanced away but answered her unspoken question. "They were sold when my parents died."

"I'm sorry."

"We needed the money to settle their debts. And for the headstones."

The stillness in the kitchen and the silence between them buzzed. She told herself not to ask but then she did. He laced his hands on the countertop, seemingly relaxed until she noticed his knuckles going white.

She thought back. She had been young. But she remembered the boy in school who had lost his parents. It had frightened her to know that parents could be lost.

"It was an auto accident. Is that right?"

He nodded. "A trailer hitch failed. It was attached to a pickup truck coming in the opposite direction down Apache Trail, one of the steeper grades. They still don't know why it let go. But it did."

Morgan winced at the image her mind furnished.

"They were killed instantly. Both of them."

"I remember something about it." She'd been in second grade, so Ray had been in third. An eight-year-old, two years younger than Lisa and orphaned. This man knew exactly what Lisa would go through if anything happened to her. So did Morgan—they'd both lost parents in auto accidents. She marveled at Kenshaw Little Falcon's selection for her protector. The man had every reason to fight for her.

"I remember hearing. You lived with the Hatch family afterward." Yeager's mother and father and their son, who had died in Iraq. "I'm so sorry for your loss." She placed a hand over his joined ones.

"It was a long time ago."

"That doesn't matter. I lost my mom almost four years ago and I still miss her every day. There are so many things I want to ask her, about Lisa and…" She stopped talking, met his gaze and they came to a silent understanding. Who among the living ever escaped this kind of loss?

"I don't trust life anymore and live accordingly."

"You mean you don't take it for granted?"

"No. I mean that it's unpredictable and vicious. I don't plan for a future because I don't expect to ever see one. I know people think of me as reckless and impulsive. Maybe I am."

She had heard of his reputation but she also judged by what she saw. With her and with her daughter Ray had been nothing but stable and thoughtful. With her, Ray was a man to be trusted with precious things, like her life and the life of her daughter.

"That's why Kenshaw chose me. Because he knows I will do whatever it takes to keep you safe."

"I believe that."

He moved his hand to capture hers. His palm was warm, dry and callused. She imagined those rough hands skimming over her body and just managed to resist the shiver of longing.

"What does this have to do with the painted yellow rectangle with your birthday?" he asked.

"It's a cattle tag. The kind that goes in their ear. One of our new heifers has a marker with the same number as my birthday. My dad named her Morgan II."

Heifers were young females who had not yet calved. Morgan recalled that this particular girl would be bred for the first time this summer if she put on enough weight.

Ray squeezed her hand and then drew back, a satisfied smile on his face. "So we look there in the morning."

"But how could my father have chased down that heifer. He was weak."

"Yearlings go into the chute for vaccinations between four and twelve months. Your dad is always there to help. He could have gotten to her then."

"When is that?" she asked.

"January."

"A month before the shooting. He was still getting around then. He didn't seem ill." But he had been ill. She frowned at the thought.

"Timing is right," said Ray.

Morgan had another concern. "We don't have

a chute. How are we getting to her? Just wander out in the herd?"

"I have a better idea. Jack and his brother Carter used to be fair at calf roping. I'll ask Jack to meet us."

Jack Bear Den looked big enough to drop a full-grown cow on her side, and in a year, this heifer should be nearly 800 pounds.

Ray stood and tucked his stool at the counter. "We best get some rest."

She was certain she would get little. Between her father's death, the distraction of knowing this virile man slept under her roof and the notion of an honest to goodness treasure hunt looming.

They couldn't go tonight because she would never leave Lisa alone and she did not wish to endanger her by bringing her out into the night.

"How will we be sure we are not followed?"

"Tribal police will help." He set his empty water glass in the sink and followed her down the hall. She told herself to just say good-night and make a hasty exit, but instead she paused by her door, wondering what he would say if she invited him in. But she wouldn't ask, not with her daughter there in the next room.

"Well, thank you, Ray, for everything."

"Sure." He lifted a hand and stroked her cheek, pausing for an instant to cup her jaw. Did he want her, too?

His hand fell away and he backed into her father's room. The one her father would never return to again.

She just managed to get into her room before the tears started again.

What a mess, she thought and tumbled into her bed alone.

THE NEXT MORNING, after dropping Lisa and Cookie off with her uncle Agustin and Ray's trusted friend Dylan, she and Ray headed to tribal police headquarters. There they found Jack, who had abandoned his blazer and turquoise bolo in favor of jeans and a flannel shirt, boots and a gray cowboy hat with a colorful turquoise and silver hatband. He stood before a red pickup hitched to a trailer containing two horses.

"Ready to ride?" he asked.

She and Ray climbed in the truck and they headed out away from the tribe's cattle.

"It's the wrong direction," she said.

"Yup," said Jack. Then he lifted the radio on his hip. "Anything, chief?" he asked.

"You got company. I got them."

Jack turned onto a road that would loop back in the direction they needed to travel. They passed a tribal police car and Jack waved out the window. Then he turned to her.

"In case we have more company."

They rode in silence to the tribal cattle herd. Finding Morgan's heifer would be like finding a particular rock in a stream. Except her heifer had not yet calved. That should narrow the search.

The radio at Jack's hip sounded as tribal police chief Tinnin started talking.

"Guy Heron. Neighbor of Ms. Hooke's."

"I got one, too," said another voice.

"That's Wetselline. The officer we passed," said Jack to Ray.

"Friend of yours, Ray," said Wetselline. "Name's Andrew Peck."

Ray growled. "How's he out already?"

"No priors. Anglo. The judge set bail and he posted."

"He broke into her house," said Ray.

"And he'll be tried. Until then he's out."

"I'm going to have to crack open his skull."

"Arrest him for trespassing," said Jack into the radio. "Hold him until I get there."

"I'm escorting Heron home," said Chief Tinnin. "Out."

Jack turned to Morgan, wedged between his massive thigh and Ray's muscular one.

"You are a very popular woman, Ms. Hooke."

And she would be until they found that money. At the grazing area for the castrated males and the unbred female yearlings, Ray and Jack moved like the military unit they'd once been a part of. The horses were unloaded, bridled and mounted. Her job was to help spot Criollo cattle as they drove them by. She'd been given a can of red marking paint and been stationed at the gate between pastures. The plan was to move the cattle through the narrow gate, giving her a chance to see her heifer and use the can to mark her. The men got the herd moving and she ignored the cows with calves and the young males, easily spotted because of their trimmed horns, as she watched for the familiar numbers of any heifers. There were three that had the number twelve on their tags and had a calf. She marked them all. By the time they were done, she was covered with dust but they had three possible heifers. Ray scouted the candidates and found the correct one. Then Morgan sat back and watched in appreciation as Ray easily roped the bovine's head and Jack got a loop around a back leg. The two of them brought her down to her side, neatly hobbling her front and back hooves. When she was down, they called Morgan over. They all inspected the tag and found nothing unusual.

"Dead end," said Jack.

"No," said Ray who had squatted and got his face nearly on the ground. "Flip her."

The two men rolled the struggling heifer to her opposite side and they all looked at the horn, spotting the marks that had been etched in the smooth pale surface and then made distinct with some kind of ink.

"My father must have known that I couldn't locate this alone," she said.

"So he wanted you to find help," said Jack.

Male help, she knew. Her father's way of ensuring that she would have a man, possibly of her choosing, to assist her. Her track record in that department left much to be desired, which was why her dad had enlisted Kenshaw's help. And they had found Ray.

"What does it say?" asked Jack.

They all stared at the marks. There was a capital letter *B* followed by a vertical line and then another capital letter *B*: B |B

"What is that supposed to mean?" asked Ray.

Morgan smiled because she knew exactly where to go next.

Chapter Thirteen

"A brand?" asked Ray, hazarding a guess as he looked at the mark etched in the horn of the struggling bovine.

They were still thinking cattle and in a way they were right.

"Yes and no," she said.

Morgan took Ray aside and told him what the clue meant. The B Bar B was the brand of a ranch here in the 1920s. It had been part of the land swap that had granted them their reservation, allowing them to leave the Salt River Apache Indian Reservation where their people had been forced in the 1870s. In 1910 and again in 1930 they were granted land. But the chimney of one of the more famous rancheros remained on the reservation.

"I used to camp there with my parents. My dad collected willow and devil's claw by the stream there."

Ray knew that Morgan's father was a talented

basket man weaving bulbous olla baskets, trays and storage containers of white willow with figures of animals and men crafted from strips of black made from the pods of devil's claw. His work had been sought after by collectors and had supported his family until his illness made it impossible for him to collect materials, let alone weave.

"So this is the mark on a chimney?" Ray asked, clarifying.

"Yes. Up along the stream. All that is left is the chimney and above the mantel is a letter *B* and a bar and below that another *B*. B Bar B."

"And he stashed the money there?" asked Ray.

"I think so." Morgan looked at the calf, bawling beside its struggling mother. "When could he have possibly done this?"

Ray motioned to the calf. "Fresh brand and ear tag on that little fellow. Branding is in March. Was Karl here for that?"

Morgan shook her head. "He was arrested that day in February. So when did he etch that horn?"

"Does he help out with the tribe's herd?"

"Yes. He's good friends with our livestock manager. Or, I mean, he was." She felt the weight of her father's death like a blow.

"Well the calves are branded and tagged in September. He'd have had a chance then."

"So long ago?" She couldn't believe he had planned a murder and all this way back then.

"Or in January when they give the yearlings vaccinations."

That was more likely. She found herself nodding. "Possibly."

She wondered how long ago he repainted Lisa's statue and when he etched that first clue in his bracelet. Perhaps she'd never know.

"How far a walk up the canyon is that chimney?"

"Three or four miles and uphill. It's past the lower ruins in the box canyon."

"I've never seen it."

"You have to know where to look."

Ray helped Jack release the Heifer before returning to her. "We'll use Jack's horses. I need to get some gear, food, and extra water."

Water was the most important of supplies, as the canyon had only one spring and that was above the remains of the ranch.

He glanced at the sky. The morning was long gone and the afternoon had now crept toward evening. "Gonna be close."

"I'd like to check on Lisa."

He nodded and they headed for the trailer, already loaded and ready to roll. They drove away from town, deeper into the reservation backcountry, off-limits to outsiders without a permit. Near the top of one hill they pulled off because this was one place they all knew had cell-phone service.

She got a hold of Lisa, who had been baking with her aunt, helped take care of the baby goats with Uncle Agustin and Dylan Tehauno had apparently taught her daughter how to throw a Frisbee, of all things.

"We used to do that in Iraq," said Ray. "Ask her if he can still catch it behind his back on his index finger."

Yes, he could, Lisa reported. Morgan spoke to her uncle, who assured her that Lisa could sleep in the guest bedroom and would be waiting for her in the morning. Then he told Morgan to be careful. She planned to do that.

They continued on to the drop-off point where Morgan was surprised to see their shaman waiting with camping gear and supplies. Jack gave Ray a radio.

"You might make it before dark," said Jack. "But best not to take the horses down after sunset. Dangerous. We'll leave my truck and trailer here. Radio in to let us know your status, not your location or anything else you don't want the world to know. If we don't hear from you every few hours, we'll send in help."

The reminder that they were faced with dangers far beyond rattlesnakes and potential falls sobered

Morgan and took away the joy she had felt at the prospect of riding out alone with Ray.

Morgan checked the girth of her borrowed mare and found it tight. She needed no help to mount. Behind her in the saddlebags were their food, water and cooking kit. A tightly rolled wool blanket had been tied behind the saddle's cantle. She would be sleeping under it and the stars right next to Ray Strong. Now that was a thought that stirred her up more than strong coffee mixed with whiskey.

A campfire, starlight and a long, cool April night. She glanced at Ray who met her speculative gaze with one of his own.

"You ready?" he asked.

"You bet."

HAD RAY BEEN imagining the desire blazing in Morgan's deep brown eyes? He sure hoped so, but his mind would not let him rest and his body made it difficult to sit in his saddle. He took point and glanced back often, mostly just to enjoy the sight of her, hips swaying with the rocking movement of the saddle and the sunlight caressing her flushed skin. Had he really ever thought she looked like a lost child?

She seemed all woman now, with her chin up and her mouth curved in a knowing smile.

"Almost there," she promised.

They rode along the gradual incline of the wide stream past the towering oak trees that shaded their way. This was good grazing land with plenty of water. He spotted the remains of the fence posts still visible and still clinging to the rusting coils of barbed wire. He might have missed the place that had once been a wide road, had Morgan not brought it to his attention. He had been to the ruins, farther up the canyon, but somehow he had never seen the chimney she mentioned. When they reached it, he understood why. Wild grapes nearly engulfed the standing masonry. Just the top eight feet of the chimney showed—exposed red brick of what had once protruded from the roof of a ranch house. The hearth itself was wide and open.

They dismounted and Ray used Jack's radio to call in, reporting on the weather. Morgan tied their horses, drank some water and then offered the canteen to Ray. He accepted the vessel and lifted his head to drink. She was mesmerized by the rhythmic up-and-down movement of his Adam's apple and the way he used the back of his forearm to wipe away the moisture that clung to his mouth. By the time he stowed the canteen, Morgan's skin tingled all over and there was a steady, insistent throbbing low and deep.

She gave herself a mental shake and left him to search the chimney. It had been years since she had made this trip, before Lisa was born, she realized. Back when she was no more than a girl herself and life seemed richer and more full of promise.

Morgan tugged back the hearty vines to reveal the marks as Ray made his way to her. In the redbrick column, the maker had added a gray-stone *B*. Beneath was a four-inch piece of similar stone and below that another capital letter *B*.

"Never saw this before," he said.

They looked in the chimney and felt around but found nothing that could be a secreted box of money. Finally, sweating and with bits of grapevine clinging to their hair, they stepped back.

Morgan spotted it first and gave a little cry of surprise.

"There!" she pointed at the side of the chimney. The stones inside the hearth had been blackened from many fires. But someone had used a stone to pound away a design in the same manner by which the petroglyphs had been created on the face of the dark basalt stone cliffs by ancient people.

Ray examined the images. They were just the right height for someone sitting in the hearth and the rounded stone used to make the pattern still lay in the hearth.

"They look recent," said Ray.

Morgan lifted the stone tool and gave a gasp. "My father's mark."

She held the stone and he saw the capital *K* and the shape of a fishing hook. Karl Hooke. Ray recognized the insignia that her father had included on the rim of all his baskets using a banded pattern of black devil's claw and white willow. And there was the same mark scratched on the side of the pestle Karl had used.

"He made this," she said, her fingers reverently stroking the mark. Then she turned her attention to the petroglyph her father had knocked into the wall of the hearthstone in a series of taps so that the pattern seemed to be created with a machinist's ball-peen hammer instead of a stone. Ray studied the engraving, thinking it looked like many he had seen in various places on the reservation and elsewhere in the southwest. The symbols showed two turtles and a crane. Morgan nodded and a smile played across her mouth.

"I know these marks."

"It's a location?" he asked.

"The upper ruins. It's on a stone in the cliff dwelling."

On the ride in, they had passed the lower ruins, which were a series of stone mounds and the walls that once formed the lower rooms of red stone and oak-framed communal homes. This was all that remained of a pueblo people who came before them. Ray knew the place, of course.

Then there were the upper ruins left by the ancient ones who had lived here a thousand years before the Apache and left for reasons of their own. Their home had been built of stone that had been carefully laid into the natural cave. The water came from the spring at the foot of the cliff, which was hauled up the cliff face in clay pots tied with cordage made from willow. There were pots still up there, untouched by their people and yet undiscovered by pot hunters, the looters who saw only money when they looked at the possessions of the ancient ones. Perhaps her father had left her the money in one of those pots. Ray hoped so, because his next call confirmed that the treasure hunters were becoming bolder.

They checked in again and Jack told him that the patrol had turned away two more vehicles. One of the shops in Darabee was selling maps with the location of Morgan's home and the museum where some of her father's baskets had been available were now sold out. Jack reported that the one large olla basket in the tribe's museum, also made by her father, had been stolen and recovered. Ray stowed the radio and they prepared the horses to resume their journey.

The upper ruins resided high in a natural cave in the rock face. Reaching it took climbing skills and a complete absence of the fear of heights. He gave Morgan a speculative look.

"What?" she asked.

"You've been up there?"

"Of course. Many times."

"Into the kivas?" he asked, referring to the circular chambers built high up on the cliff face into the natural cave by the ancients for religious ceremonies.

"What are you asking, Ray?"

"You seemed like the both-feet-on-the-ground kind of girl. Risk averse and definitely not a pot hunter."

"I'm no pot hunter. But I'm a good climber. If you are careful, it doesn't have to be dangerous."

He grinned. "Keep telling yourself that. Everything is dangerous. This stream cut these canyons. Those logs were thrown up on the bank during flash floods from storms farther up. Lightning strikes. Rattlesnake bites. Horses can roll on you." He patted the side of the Appaloosa who did not slow his steady gate.

"Trail hitches fail," she said.

He met her gaze, seeing an understanding of him that gave him a chill.

He nodded. "Deer in the road."

"You never expected to make it this far, did you?" she asked.

Ray shook his head. "It's freeing, in a way. Not

expecting to survive. It gives you a kind of courage to try things. From the outside it might look like recklessness or bravery. But it's really a lack of faith and an understanding that none of us can expect a future. Planning for it seems counterintuitive."

"I couldn't live like that. I have a child. So I don't take risks and I plan for her future."

He nodded. "I can understand that."

"You're good with her, you know? My daughter."

What did that mean? Was she trying him on for size as a potential father to her girl? Ray surprised himself by not feeling an immediate rejection of the thought. Instead he was gripped with something unfamiliar, a kind of ache behind his breastbone. He wasn't staying around to play house. She must know that. So why was he picturing her waiting for him in the welcoming kitchen of her small home?

Morgan was more than appealing and Lisa was a wonderful kid. But he wasn't the sort of man a woman chose for a husband and father. He knew what women wanted from him and up until now that had been just fine. So what was with the ache in his chest?

He was more the sort you brought home to terrify your parents and impress your friends. The wrong kind of man for a good girl who didn't like risks.

"Lisa is a sweet kid," he said.

"And she's been through a lot."

That must be true. No father, but Ray knew that Karl had adequately filled those shoes. But he could do so no longer. Ray's mind shot him an image of his parents' graves and the single headstone they shared.

People you loved left you. Not by choice. But they were just as gone. Lisa deserved a dad. Someone like Jack or Dylan. The idea of him trying to be a father to Lisa terrified him more than his nightmares of the insurgent attack where they lost Hatch.

"We better get moving," he said.

Chapter Fourteen

Ray retrieved the horses and held her mount as she swung up into the saddle. She was a fine sight astride a horse. Made his own withers twitch as images that had no business in his mind continued to pop up like prairie dogs in a meadow.

Ray's radio crackled and he spoke to Jack, explaining their decision to spend the night. He did not give their location or any other details. Jack promised to check on Lisa and radio back. Then they were on their way. They followed a Jeep trail cut in the tall yellow grass. They rode abreast, each in one of the ruts left by the tires.

"Seems someone has been up here recently," said Ray, studying the tread marks left in the sand. Too small for a pickup, he realized. "Do you think your father was well enough to make this ride?" said Ray.

Karl had been in the last stages of his cancer.

Riding up to a cliff dwelling seemed impossibly difficult to Morgan.

"He might have used his four-wheeler for most of it. He has one as well as ramps to drive it right up into his truck."

"You said he couldn't drive."

"He wasn't supposed to drive. But the day before the shooting, he took his truck. I was on nights then. He was gone when I woke up but back before my next shift."

"You ask where he went?"

"I did. He said it was personal."

"When do you get home from work?"

"In time to get Lisa on the bus."

Ray paused, thinking. "So he was gone up to ten hours?"

"Possibly."

The sunlight now shone just on the eastern wall of the canyon, painting the rock a dazzling orange, but shadows were slowly climbing up the rock face as the sun sank.

"Do you want to camp at the base of the cliff or up in the caves?" he asked.

"Caves are better for defense," she said.

Ray lifted his brow. She was thinking like a strategist. "Sounds good. We should make it by dark. Be close though."

They took the turn along the stream past the willows that grew so thick he did not see the elk until it darted out from cover to charge up the opposite bank. They dismounted and led the horses away from the stream, taking them up the dry canyon and pausing to water them at the natural spring. Ray admired the green vegetation here by the water. There were pinyon trees and oak and an abundance of wild grape growing with broad leaves and the buds that would soon flower. But just past the spring and in all directions to the canyon walls, the ground was thirsty and the vegetation sparse, dry and yellowing.

He tied the horses and loosened the girths, but left the bridles for now. He let the horses drink as he refilled their water bottles and his canteen. They each took a few minutes alone to relieve themselves. They met by the water and washed away some of the dust from their faces.

"Your father was wise not to leave the money with you, but the clues make it unlikely that anyone could find the cash without you. That puts you and his granddaughter at risk. I know Karl well enough to know he never intended that."

"But did he really think I would keep it?"

Ray cocked his head as if this never occurred to him.

"It's blood money. If all that you and the FBI have told me is true, then he was paid this ransom to murder a man."

"A mass murderer."

"A human being."

"Who shot nine other human beings dead, including women, one of whom was pregnant."

"Sanchez was a disturbed man. But my father, he wasn't a killer."

Clearly Karl had not shared any of his war stories with his daughter. That was for the best. But Karl *had* been a killer. A darned good one. A killer and a man who wove baskets.

"Even if it wasn't illegal to keep the money, I could never spend any of it. It's just morally wrong."

"Your dad was trying to look after his family. He used what he had, a talent for shooting and the knowledge that he was not long for this world."

"I love my father, Ray. But that does not mean I condone his actions."

"He was a good man."

"But he deceived me and he knew…" She stopped talking and looked at the rock face rising to their left.

"Knew what?"

"He knew that I hate deception. After what happened to me with Lisa's father. I just can't bear people lying. He knew that and yet he did not reveal a word of his plans."

Ray's stomach clenched. He was here to protect Morgan, but that was only part of his assignment. Kenshaw had also instructed him to discover exactly what Morgan knew of her father's business. This had not bothered him when he accepted, but now that he knew her, everything was different. She'd hate him, too, when she discovered his lie of omission.

"He was protecting you."

"He hasn't protected me. He's put me and his granddaughter in danger. All because of a lie. He knew if he told me what I would say."

"You'd have tried to stop him."

"Of course I would! I'd have gone to Chief Tinnin and had him locked up. Isn't that what you do with those you love? You keep them from making mistakes—even if for the right intention, his decision was wrong."

Ray knew that he wouldn't have told her either. And he would have been a lot more careful about how he collected that cash. But then, it would not have mattered. Because Morgan would just give it all back.

"So you want to turn the money over to the FBI," he said.

"As fast as humanly possible."

"That's probably a wise move. Once they announce the recovery of the money, the wolves will leave your door. You and Lisa will be safe."

"But still broke." She laughed. "I need to get back to work at the casino or I'll need to apply to the tribe for temporary assistance."

Medical care, such as it was and Lisa's education were paid for by the tribe. Morgan might be paying rent on the tribal housing, if she could afford it. Without Karl here, the tribe might reassign them to a smaller place. Lisa would lose the only home she had ever known. Ray thought of the day he left his home to move in with Yeager's parents. He didn't know what happened to his parents' things. The adults had taken care of that.

"Ray?" Morgan asked. "Are you all right?"

"Why?"

"You just look sad."

"Karl didn't want you to lose your home."

She straightened her spine and lifted her chin. "It's just a house."

That was an admission that Morgan knew exactly what was coming. He realized that there were many challenges ahead for Morgan and her girl, small everyday struggles with everyday issues. But that was only if they could find this money. He looked at the sky, still blue but fading now with bands of yellow and orange creeping in from the west. They needed to get to the ruins. He glanced back.

"You think we are being followed?" asked Morgan.

"I wouldn't be surprised."

They continued along in silence, Morgan falling behind his horse as the path narrowed. If Karl had driven, he would have had to make these last two hundred yards on foot, carrying the money. Then he would have to hide it before walking back to his vehicle. And that was if he hid the money at the base of the cliff dwelling. Ray hoped they would not find another clue turning them back the way they had come.

Here the banks grew steep with red rock rising on their left. Cactus and yucca clung to the clefts along the way. And now he saw the cave some one hundred yards up the steep rocky grade. The last fifty feet was a sheer cliff face with niches carved by human hands to assist in the final ascent. He could not picture Karl making such a climb, especially not burdened with anything, like two hundred thousand dollars.

Then he and Morgan scrambled up loose rock and over red stone to the base of the cliff. He retrieved the wooden ladder that was carved in a series of notches up the trunk of a ponderosa pine. The ladder did not reach the lip of the cave, but nearly so. The last fifteen feet was made along a fissure in the rock with the assistance of niches carved by the ancient ones. Together they leaned the beam into the notch that had likely been used for a thousand years for this purpose. She headed up first, leaving Ray to admire the sight of Morgan as she climbed up and then into the fissure in the stone. The woman had not been bragging, for she climbed with the ease of a mountain goat. Once she was out of sight, he released his hold on the beam and tied their packs and saddle bags to a rope, which he tied to himself. Then he followed her.

By the time he reached the crack in the stone, she had mounted the final few feet of the steep incline that led to the cave floor. This dwelling was easy to miss from below if you did not know the location. He wondered if enemies might have walked right below the noses of the people living in the caves above. The place was very defensible. There were poles in the caves cut to a length that could knock the pine ladder away. If an enemy was climbing to the rim of the cave, it would be easy to knock that enemy off the ledge with falling stones or the strike of a club.

But there were two vulnerabilities. First, there was no water in the caves, so an enemy might wait them out. It seemed that a historic drought did drive the ancient ones away. The second weakness was the exposed lip of the cave floor that protruded from the cliff face, making it possible to roll rocks down from above.

Morgan called down from above that she had reached the top. Ray concentrated on placing a hand and then a foot into the notches carved in the sandstone wall. Each had three grooves, worn from the fingers of thousands of men and women who had climbed before him. They, however, were not wearing boots. The footholds were never meant for such footgear or for a man who was over six three and wore a size twelve shoe. In this climb, a woman had the advantage. He reached the top, sweating and thirsty. Morgan offered him a hand and he took it. She hauled and he pushed until he stood on the cave floor beside her. She did not try to retrieve her hand.

"Look," she said, motioning with her free hand.

The light that had vanished from the canyon floor still clung to the lip of the canyon rim, turning the sandstone brilliant orange. His breath, which was already coming fast from his exertions, caught for a moment at the beauty of this place.

"Can you imagine seeing that sight every evening?" he asked.

She moved closer to his side and he looped an arm over her shoulder.

"It's lovely."

Her body felt just right tucked against his and in that moment of calm and peace, Ray glimpsed something he had not seen in many years, a future. He could imagine it now, the long days ahead with Morgan and her daughter, it came to him in a flash and vanished just as quickly. Crushed by his belief that future plans were for fools who did not understand that life was not to be trusted.

He stepped away.

"I'd better get our gear. The light's fading." He hauled their packs up and together they set up camp and had a meal of cold sandwiches and water with the fresh fruit Jack had added to their things. Afterward they went to see the petroglyph Morgan recalled. There in the back of one of the rooms were the animal effigies that were nearly identical to the ones Karl had tapped into the side of the chimney. But search as they might, they found no place nearby where the floor or stone walls had been disturbed.

"A dead end," he said.

Morgan's shoulders drooped. "This means they won't stop coming."

He feared that this treasure might become like the fabled Lost Dutchman's Mine in the Superstition Mountains with entrepreneurs selling maps to treasure hunters who would invade their land as the Spanish and the Anglos had done. But worse than that, they might hurt Morgan in an attempt to find that money.

The sun sank behind them and the sky changed rapidly from orange to deep blue. Stars emerged one after another until, by the time they finished their meal, they were scattered across the heavens.

"Did you ever sleep here?" he asked.

"No. Day trips only. My dad liked to look at the petroglyphs and pottery shards. He studied the cordage to see how the ancient ones made their ropes and baskets."

"I'd prefer to be well away from the edge when we bed down," said Ray.

They had not hauled wood and so they had no fire. They sat on the ledge looking out at the stars and Ray thought this one of the most peaceful moments of his life. A silent contentment filled him as Morgan spoke about coming here with her father as a girl.

"His favorite glyphs are those the ancient ones used as calendars. He used to show us the petroglyphs and explain them. He came here a lot as a boy especially at the equinox. He said there was a mark for each one."

"To mark the solstices and equinoxes?" he asked.

"Yes and the times to plant the crops."

Ray looked back toward the wall of markings. "I'd like to see that."

"It's down below. There's a rock whose shadow points to the markings when the sun crests the eastern canyon wall. It lines up perfectly for each planting time."

"And your father showed you this?"

She nodded.

"Morgan, maybe that's where he left the next clue."

"Should we go down there?"

"You think you can make that climb in the dark?"

She nodded and they gathered up their supplies. Ray lowered them to the ground and went first. Morgan climbed down behind him and they reached the canyon floor in only a few minutes.

"Easier in the dark," she said. "You can still see the hand holds but you're not distracted by the height."

For a woman who loved security and didn't take risks, Morgan was certainly doing a good impression of a daredevil.

MORGAN LED HIM a short distance along the cliff face. Around them, the familiar shrubs and brush cast long shadows in the starlight. There was more than enough light to see and she found the place easily.

Ray studied the swirling spirals and series of descending lines that reminded Ray of a staircase.

"That's the planting schedule. When the shadow from the tip of that rock—" she pointed to a jagged rock that had split from the main canyon wall in some long-ago time "—falls on this mark, it tells the people to plant their first crop. Here's the second and the third, which was cotton. Over there, each of the spirals marks one of the solstices or equinoxes. The whole thing is an elaborate calendar."

"Where does the shadow fall now?" Ray asked.

Morgan turned to him, seeming to know his mind. She smiled. "I guess we will find out tomorrow."

They laid out the bedrolls so that they would be here beside the wall at first light. Morgan moved her bedroll closer to his and settled in. He excused himself and when he returned it was to the soft breathing of a sleeping woman. He tried to tell himself it was for the best. That this woman was special and she deserved a man who could love her for a lifetime. He could protect her. But he was not the sort of dependable man who could help her make a home. He remembered his parents. But they had left him when he was so young. He had no clue how to be a father to Lisa, who would be preparing for her sunrise ceremony in only a year. Morgan should have a dependable, reliable man of honor. That was what she needed. Not one who had a prior for rolling his car in Darabee, an event he could not even remember because he'd been so drunk. Not a love affair. Not another man to leave her. She needed a man who would stay forever.

He lay awake beside her, watching the stars gently wheel across the sky and the moon crest the top of the canyon. Morgan rolled toward him, giving him a view of her sleeping face. He felt blessed that she trusted him enough to sleep beside him. He didn't deserve it, of course. He was to be trusted no more than any man and less than some because he wanted what any male would want, and he'd deceived her. Ray had not told her about his mission from Kenshaw to see what she knew of her father's business.

He felt like a traitor and wished he could be the kind of man she deserved.

MORGAN ROUSED IN the night in a panic, unsure where she was. Ray was there in an instant whispering reassurances and gathering her close. She laid her head on the pillow of his arm and rolled to her back, staring up at the sparkling curtain of stars visible between the gap of the canyon walls. If there was a more beautiful sight, she had never seen it.

"Lovely," she whispered.

He made a humming noise that rumbled through his chest. Then he kissed the top of her head. She lifted her chin and the next kiss dropped on her willing mouth. Morgan slid a knee up over his muscular thigh as the kiss blossomed into something warm and sensual.

Ray's mouth moved to graze his teeth against the sensitive skin of her neck as her hands worked up under his shirt to the strong cording muscles of his back. She raked her nails down his flesh and heard his intake of breath. His mouth met hers and he deepened the kiss, their tongues gliding over each other as his fingers caressed her.

He broke away to lift her blouse and kiss her stomach, each swirl of his tongue bringing her sensitized flesh alive and triggering a pulsing want that only he could satisfy.

"Ray?"

His dark head lifted and he stared up at her, his eyes hooded and mysterious.

"Don't stop."

His grip tightened as if he wanted to possess her, but he did not move, just stared up at her.

"Are you sure?" he asked. He seemed to be holding his breath as he awaited her answer.

She nodded. "I'm certain."

Ray's smile was devilish and now her breath caught as he unbuttoned her blouse and slid it from her shoulders. He followed by tugging off his shirt and T-shirt together. Then he turned his attention to the tops of her breasts exposed above the lace of her white bra. His delicious hot breath fanned her desire and she lifted to unclasp the bra, adding it to his discarded clothing. He paused to look at her and she found his gaze stirred her as much as his touch. He had told her that this was a job to him, but this, what they now shared, she knew it was real. She also knew it would not last. Nothing this good ever did. Not for her anyway.

He stroked the skin at her collarbone as he

moved in to kiss her breasts. Her body reacted with heat, growing wet and ready. But he took his time, exploring her thoroughly before moving downward. When he moved back up to take her mouth, her boots, socks, jeans and panties had been cast aside and she could taste herself on his lips. She was ready but Ray rolled away. It gave her a moment to think about what she was doing. It didn't make her change her mind but served only to convince her how much she wanted him, if only once.

When he returned to her it was to offer the slim, slippery foil package that showed either his willingness to protect her or his desire to safeguard himself from unwanted encumbrances. She tore open the packet and together they slipped on the sheath. Her hands shook in her eagerness.

"It's been a long time," she said, nervous and wanting all at once.

He smiled and she knew it had not been a long time for him. Men like Ray were never without female company unless they chose to be. She needed to remember that. But in a moment she was in his arms again and her qualms slipped away. She didn't care about tomorrow. Only tonight and Ray and the heat and the friction and the bliss.

Chapter Fifteen

Ray woke with the birdsong. Morgan lay tucked up against his side, her bare back and bottom pressed against him, warming him. He threw an arm over his forehead and grew aroused all over again at the memories of Morgan in his arms. She was not the sort of lover he'd expected. He assumed she would be subdued and gentle. But Morgan was a hunting puma and her fire thrilled him. He had been with enough women to know the difference. He and Morgan had a rare chemistry and syncopation that made him hungry to have her again.

But now, in her slumber, all the cares and worries she bore faded. He saw the perfect peace and otherworldly beauty that he had no business trying to possess. Even if he longed for this kind of woman, he didn't deserve her and had no faith that she would want a broken man haunted by ghosts.

Ray roused from his bedroll, tossing away the

blanket with disgust. He had some nerve messing with a single mother. Some nerve.

Still he glanced back at her, the blankets now at her hips. He reached for her and then stopped, fisting his hand and forcing himself to leave her be.

The sun was up but had not yet risen over the eastern lip of the canyon when Ray had the fire going and the coffee on. That roused Morgan, who yawned and sat up to stretch in a way that made Ray drop one of the tin coffee cups. He caught it on the second bounce and found Morgan smiling at him. The look of satisfaction she held in her dark eyes made him feel only marginally better about his breach of protocol.

"I'm starving," she said. "What's for breakfast?"

"Morgan, I want to apologize for last night."

Her smile faded and the worry lines returned to her forehead. Some of the beauty vanished like moisture into the dry air.

"Apologize?"

"I don't want you to think that what happened last night changes anything between us." In fact, sex changed everything between a man and woman. He knew it and from the confusion in her eyes, she knew it, too. "I'm still your protector. I'll stay as long as I'm needed. But…"

She snorted. "We slept together, Ray. You didn't ask me to marry you."

Now he was wondering what she would say if he did ask. *No* would be the wisest reply. *Hell no*, even better.

"Yeah. I know. But women read things into such encounters. I didn't want you to do that."

"Encounters." She fastened her bra, drawing the lace over her breasts, before yanking on her blouse and finally, tugging on her jeans. Next she slid bare feet into hiking boots and headed for the privacy of the brush. But she turned like a cornered animal to face him. "I never asked you for any sort of commitment, Ray. I'm a big girl and certainly don't need you to explain to me how the world works."

She left his sight and a moment later he heard a familiar rattle that could only come from a coiled rattlesnake. Such snakes gained a rattle each time they shed their skin and the sound of this rattle told him it was a damn big one.

"Morgan?"

She did not answer.

"Don't move. I'm coming."

He found her standing stock-still facing a coiled rattler that had its back against the rock face and had no way to escape but by lunging at Morgan. Ray had a pistol in his boot, but they were too imprecise. The rifle was back at camp.

Ray drew out his knife. Morgan's eyes moved but she wisely remained motionless. The snake continued to rattle a warning. Ray usually let snakes be, but there was no way to this time because Morgan had inadvertently cornered the reptile and now stood in striking distance. If he got close enough to use a stick to pin the head, it might just lash out at Morgan's leg and hit her above her boot.

"Don't back up. Don't move. Run when I hit it," he said. Ray would have to be quick as a mongoose. He adjusted his grip on the knife, taking hold of the wide, flat blade. One of his favorite pastimes as a boy and then in Iraq was throwing this particular knife. He was accurate at twenty paces. But he'd never had a woman's life hanging in the balance. Not just any woman, but Morgan.

And now she had become so much more.

Don't think. Just do it.

He lifted the weapon. The snake's tongue flicked and the rattling increased in tempo. Ray threw.

"Run!"

Morgan sprang away like an antelope. But it was unnecessary. The snake's head had been severed from its writhing body. Ray watched the blood drain and the snake's body come to eventual rest.

"All I could think of was Lisa," Morgan said as she now clung to him. "I just want to get that money back to the FBI and go home."

Ray allowed himself to hold her until she stopped trembling. After checking the area to be sure there were no more snakes, he left her to finish her business.

He used the radio to call Jack and then checked on the horses, walking them down to the spring, then back to the camp to find Morgan, pale but composed. Her eyes seemed a little redder than he recalled. He hoped she had not been crying or if she had been that she wouldn't start up again. What the heck had he been thinking last night?

Ray snorted. Thinking was not what he'd been doing. And just like always, this Eagle Warrior spotted trouble too late. He didn't know what to say or do about their little encounter. But in truth, he was already thinking about how to do it again.

Man, he was low.

They ate breakfast and broke camp as the sun rose higher, nearing midmorning and the time it would make its appearance over the canyon ridge.

"This is where we used to sit. My father said that rock was the one that the ancient people used." She pointed to the wall of stone that had separated from the rest of the rock on the canyon's face. The sun had finally reached the ridge, sending rays of light across the eastern wall, gradually inching down the cliff dwelling and closer to their position. They were only a little past the spring equinox but he could see where the one spiral was very near to the place the shadow now fell. The other spirals showed how far the shadow traveled through the year.

"There," she said. "See how it has gone past the first two dots on that line? That means the first two plantings are over and it isn't yet time to sow the cotton seeds. That was the third crop. After that it's beans and squash and pumpkin."

Ray watched the shadow crawl across the canyon wall as he sipped bitter black coffee from his mug and he made a guess as to where the shadow would fall when it met the earth. There he saw a pile of stones that did not look as if they had been arranged by nature. Could Karl have expected them to follow this trail and to be here in the month of April? Did he know so well the shadow's path and when he would die and when Morgan would follow those clues? The small hairs lifted on his neck and he knew that Karl had planned it all.

"Morgan. Look at that pile of stones."

She did and her mouth dropped open as she put the pieces together. Then she shivered. "Do you think?"

"I do."

They moved to the pile, preceding the shadow that moved quickly now as the sun rose higher. They moved the stones, one by one, and found a green plastic cooler half buried in the dry soil. Ray looked at Morgan who sat back on her heels.

"That's it, isn't it?" she whispered.

"Do you recognize this?"

"Yes. My father's. I didn't notice it was missing."

Ray lifted the lid, knowing what he would find. He was not disappointed. The small cooler, designed to hold six cans of liquid instead held stacks of bills, neatly tied with long strands of buffalo grass that had just begun to yellow.

Morgan tilted her head back until she looked straight up at the sky as if she could not look at the money. Ray left the lid open as he watched her. They sat behind the line of shadow but the canyon wall now blazed with light.

She shaded her eyes. "What's that?"

He followed the direction of her gaze and saw something dark in the gap between the two canyon walls. It did not soar like a hawk but hovered like a hummingbird, soundless and three hundred feet or more above them. Ray snapped the lid of the cooler shut.

"Drone," he said.

"A drone? You mean one of those things that fly around and interfere with aircraft?"

"I have to call this in." He was on his feet as the drone veered out of sight.

"Is it from the FBI?"

He sure hoped so. "No way to tell."

Ray radioed in and told Jack what had happened. Jack said he'd call Luke Forrest and that he was on his way with back up.

"Get to the horses," Ray said.

"Are we taking the money?" she asked.

Great question. Because either with or without the money, they were bound to meet trouble.

"I got it." He yanked the cooler free and tied it to the cantle of his saddle. Then he checked his rifle to be sure it was loaded and ready. Morgan bridled the horses and secured their bedrolls. With the horses saddled and the girths tight, the two mounted up to begin the ride down the canyon.

They met trouble before they even left camp.

RAY'S FIRST INDICATION of company came when the bedrock at his feet exploded. He recognized a rifle shot but his horse went crazy, rearing on his hind legs and continuing over. Ray had been on enough horses to know his mount was going over backward and leaped from the saddle, landing beside the rolling horse as the spine of the saddle cracked.

"Ray!" Morgan leaned from her saddle, extending her hand for him and he was about to accept her hand when he realized the money and his rifle were tied to his saddle.

Another shot sent rock shards up beside his

boots. Ray drew the pistol from his boot holster and turned in the direction of fire.

"Drop it, soldier, or I drop her."

Ray didn't, of course and the next shot was fired. Her horse screamed and fell to its front knees, sending Morgan tumbling over the withers and onto the ground. Her horse struggled to his feet, his fetlock gushing blood.

"Next one takes her life," called the shooter.

Ray threw his pistol aside and moved to Morgan.

"Radio," said the shooter.

Ray dropped his only means of communication. Cell phones were useless up here. The man motioned him back and then moved in to smash the radio with a rock while Ray thought about his knife. It was a straight blade, about four inches. The right sort for cutting a rope or throwing at a man's chest.

"Walk this way," called their attacker.

Ray helped Morgan rise and they walked in the direction of the bullets. A man stepped out from cover. He was dressed for riding in a denim jacket, wide brimmed hat, jeans and boots. His hair was dark and he needed a shave. The Anglo was about fifty and had a badge clipped to his belt.

"You're on tribal land," said Ray.

"I know where I am, Strong," came the reply.

Morgan gasped. "I've seen you before," she said.

"I was afraid of that. Avoided you at the station when we brought you in."

"You brought me in?"

"My guys. I'm the chief of police in Darabee."

Ray took another look. It had been a while since he'd met Jefferson Rowe, but he remembered him.

For just a moment Morgan looked relieved while Ray judged the distance he'd need to throw the knife and found it too far. He had to bury that blade to the hilt and he didn't expect that Chief Rowe would allow him close and personal enough to stick him.

"Well, Ray Strong. Been a long time." He laughed.

Rowe had been the arresting officer the night Ray had rolled his truck in Darabee with a blood alcohol level that should have rendered him unconscious which at the time seemed preferable to his grief over Hatch. That was no crime. But then he'd picked up his keys and driven his truck. He deserved what followed—every bit of it.

"Are you here to arrest us?" she asked.

"Not exactly. If you wouldn't mind getting Ray's horse? And please don't touch his rifle or I'll shoot him where he stands."

Morgan left them to do exactly what Rowe ordered.

"You a private contractor now, Rowe?" Ray asked.

"Sure beats a cop's pension."

Morgan returned leading Ray's Appaloosa gelding. Rowe motioned for her to come nearer, keeping the rifle aimed at Ray. She advanced slowly, showing the caution she had said she lived by. But if that were true, then when she had been out of sight up the canyon, she could have kept on going. Instead she had returned with his horse, which seemed uninjured, and placed herself right back in Rowe's sights.

"They're really worried about you, Morgan. What your father told you. What you know. If you can identify the man who paid your dad off."

Ray realized that the chief of police would make a valuable operative for the eco-extremists.

He hazarded a guess. "Would that be the same man who made sure her dad knew exactly when and where he'd have a clean shot at Ovidio Sanchez?"

"Very good, Mr. Strong. I see you are not always pickled in alcohol."

"I saw you in the restaurant that day," said Morgan. "You held the door for me."

"See, I knew you held eye contact a little too long. Did you recognize me from the station? I was careful not to be the one to interview you after your dad's arrest."

Morgan shook her head.

"Well, shoot. But you did spot me after I

dropped off the check. You understand my reason for concern?"

"You work for BEAR?" she asked.

"See? You shouldn't even know the name of that outfit. Bears are dangerous, child. So, I can safely report that you do know what organization hired your father."

"Because the FBI questioned me about them."

"And that I was hired by BEAR. You know any of their names?"

She shook her head.

"Not sure I believe you. I know they won't. Skittish as cattle at a slaughterhouse, that group."

"But I don't know them," she said.

"Doesn't matter. What matters is that they think you know them. That you were your father's confidante. They are aware of your visit to your dad the day he passed."

"He was unconscious," said Ray.

"Not all day. They have information. And you were both there. This group doesn't take chances."

"But you stood by while they collected a great deal of explosives," said Morgan.

"That's not true. I protected them. Transported goods and kept them all safe. Now I'm planning a retirement in Alaska. Should be far enough away to avoid the crater they'll make. They have nearly unlimited funds thanks to all those bleeding hearts who want to restore the wild. They never show the blood on the claws of the tigers in the fund-raising videos or the elk with shredded hamstrings thanks to those newly reintroduced wolves."

"What are they blowing up, Jefferson?" asked Ray.

"Don't know. Don't care. I've got enough money to get while the getting is good. Hope they blow up Las Vegas. I hate that wart on the desert. Or New York. Gray buildings. Cold and rainy most days, and when the sun comes out, it stinks like garbage. We'd be doing them a favor. Believe me. Don't even get me started on LA. They're pampered poodles with affluenza up the ying-yang. Spend $100 K to protect tree frogs and step right over the homeless veterans on their way to their limos." Rowe spat.

"So are you are here for the money or to see what Morgan knows?" asked Ray.

"Both. Kind of a win-win."

"Your drone?" asked Ray.

"Theirs. It's a loaner. They have such cool toys. Been watching you two." He rubbed the top of the barrel with an index finger in a shame-shame motion.

Morgan's cheeks flamed and Ray clamped his teeth so tight they squeaked.

"And here I thought you were a nice girl," he

said to Morgan. "You turned me down a time or two at the casino."

Her eyes widened in remembrance. "You were at the casino the night before the shooting."

"That's right. I'd handed your papa a big fat check a few days before and dropped by to see his little girl had quit her job yet. But you were still there. Made me think you two weren't as close as I thought. He didn't tell you about it before hand. Did he? Must have done that after because he'll never live to spend it. But I sure plan to. Nice of him to cash that check for me." He glanced at Ray. "Now, I figure the FBI is en route and Detective Bear Den is already on his way up the canyon. So I better scoot."

"He'll see you coming down," said Ray.

"See me? Hell, boy, he called me for backup. Your tribal police only got three or four guys on duty on a good day. Plus I'm closer to the ruins than they are up in Pinyon Forks. I just got here sooner."

"How will you explain the money? I told him we found it."

"You think he'll search me or look for your killers?"

Ray knew the answer. Jack would take the lawman at his word and come searching. He hoped that Rowe didn't plan to hurt Jack. He slipped his fingers around the grip of his knife, thinking he was running out of time. Funny, for a long time after he came back from Iraq he really hadn't cared if he lived or died. The unnecessary risks told him he was leaning toward dying. But not now.

Now death had found him and he wanted to live to protect Morgan.

"Pull that knife and I shoot you first," said Rowe. Then he turned to Morgan. "Drop the reins and step back."

She dropped the reins and stepped back. Rowe reached to take hold of the bridle as Morgan threw something. At first Ray thought it was a bit of rope, but as it sailed through the air, he recognized it as a headless rattlesnake.

An instant later the Appaloosa's eyes rolled over white.

Chapter Sixteen

Morgan dove back and rolled across the loose rock and sand, clearing the gelding's flying front feet as he tried to stomp the headless snake. Chief Rowe was not so quick and one of the hooves clipped his chest, sending him staggering back. Ray drew his knife and headed at him on a run. Rowe landed hard on his seat, regained his balance and lifted his rifle, taking aim at Morgan.

Ray threw his blade.

Because Rowe was in profile, he could not aim at his black heart but the knife did sink deep into his right side, slicing between the ribs. Rowe's shot went off target as he screamed and rolled to his uninjured side. Ray was on him a moment later, tearing the rifle from his grip and rolling to his feet above the writhing man.

Frothy blood gurgled from Rowe's mouth and Ray knew he had deflated his right lung. The chief of the Darabee police now breathed fast and shallow.

"Now you've done it," he said.

Morgan collected Ray's pistol and held it on Rowe, as well.

"Might have at least saved your little girl, Morgan. Now they'll use her as leverage to keep you quiet."

Morgan turned and ran toward Ray's fleeing horse. Ray had no doubt that she intended to gallop all the way to her uncle's home, if necessary, to get to her daughter.

"We'll tell them what you did," said Ray.

"Yeah. Go ahead. I'll tell them you stabbed me while I was trying to apprehend you. That you found the money and it made you crazy." A smile hovered on his bloody lips. "Crazier. You've always been crazy. Right, Ray? Plus you've got a criminal record. And Morgan is the daughter of an assassin, who just found her dad's blood money. Who do you think they'll believe? You or me?"

Ray backed away, uncertain now. The FBI could arrest both him and Morgan because they should have reported the information they uncovered instead of setting out alone to find the money. At the very least, they had put her daughter in more danger because with both of them in custody, who would protect Lisa?

"Well?" said Jefferson Rowe. "What are you

waiting for? If I'm dead, you're a murderer. Hard to explain away your knife in my side. So you better hope to Christ I don't bleed out before they get to me."

Ray left him, scrambling after Morgan. He needed to get Rowe medical attention and he needed to get Morgan's daughter to safety. It took a few minutes to collect the horses.

The police chief might be right that the FBI would believe his lies. But there were two factors working in Ray's favor. First, they were on Turquoise Canyon Reservation land and that meant that even the federal government had limited authority. And second, Ray had called Jack last night to report the progress of their search and again this morning to relay their discovery and the drone's appearance. It was something Jefferson Rowe could not even imagine, that Morgan wouldn't want even one dollar of that money. He had judged them on his belief system and Ray was ashamed that he had ever considered keeping what they had discovered.

Morgan's honesty might be the factor that swung the balance in their favor. Or that money might still get them killed.

Ray took charge of the horses while Morgan bandaged Jefferson's wound, leaving the knife in place to help slow the bleeding. It took both of them to get Jefferson mounted. Her horse was lame, so they left it behind. They took the pack-horse instead, though his horse's fall left Ray without a saddle. Morgan led them down and he took the position behind Jefferson.

They met a party riding four-wheelers soon after they started. Jack Bear Den lead the group, looking massive on the rugged recreational ve-hicle, wearing his familiar gray cowboy hat with the badge clipped to the ornate turquoise hat band. Behind him came three similar vehicles ridden by men and women dressed in a particular navy blue jacket with bold yellow lettering announcing that they were FBI.

Ray dismounted and went to meet the wel-coming party. Morgan fairly flew off her horse, dropping the reins to rush past him. She headed straight for Luke Forrest, the Black Mountain Apache and FBI field agent.

"My daughter. You have to get her. Right now. Please."

Forrest glanced to Jack Bear Den.

"Your daughter is already at the tribal police station."

Morgan didn't know if she should be relieved or more concerned.

"She's safe," said Forrest.

Morgan drew the first full breath since coming down from the ruins.

The other officers moved past them, heading

for the wounded man who started talking fast and loud.

"We're taking these two back to Pinyon Forks," said Forrest to his partner, Cassidy Cosen.

"I thought we were going to Darabee," said Cosen.

"We stay on tribal lands for now," said Forrest.

"Darabee is closer and Rowe needs a hospital." She turned to Ray. "Is that a knife in his ribs?"

Ray admitted that it was not only a knife but his knife.

"You are under arrest," said Cosen.

Forrest stepped in. "You accompany Rowe to the hospital," said Forrest. "Check in with me on his condition. Put a protective detail on him and make sure he stays put until I get there."

"We should bring them all to Darabee," said Cosen.

Forrest shook his head. This man understood the protection afforded Apaches while on their reservation and that those protections would end the moment they set foot off their land.

Cosen scowled but lifted her radio, calling for paramedics. Then she took charge of Jefferson Rowe, seeing him moved from the horse to the four-by-four. She and two of the agents disappeared back down the canyon.

"Now," said Forrest, "We have some questions."

MORGAN AND RAY rode in Jack's patrol car, preceded and followed by FBI.

"They sure seem like they're running the show," said Ray.

"Well they're not, because they can't take either of you unless our tribal council votes to turn you over. And they'll only consider that if you are charged with a crime they think warrants federal prosecution.

"Like stabbing the chief of police of Darabee?"

Jack made a face.

"Why did you move Lisa to the station, Jack?" asked Morgan.

"Dylan suggested it." Jack glanced at her. "You have to stay calm. Your daughter is fine."

This, of course, had the opposite effect. Her heart now hammered so loudly in her ears she could barely think, let alone hear. She held both hands pressed over her pounding heart, trying to assuage the pain and the dizziness that threatened.

Ray wrapped an arm around her and tugged her against him. "She's safe. Jack just said so."

Morgan nodded. "Safe," she whispered and squeezed her eyes shut.

"What happened?" asked Ray.

"Someone tried to grab her from the backyard of your uncle's place. Dylan got to her. She was shaken up but unharmed."

"When did this happen?" asked Ray.

"Between when we called Darabee for back up and you were found."

Ray thought about that.

"Did they catch the perp?" asked Ray.

"No. He got away. Dylan got a partial plate and a very good look at him. Young. Anglo. Hair in a man bun and with a full sandy-colored beard."

"Drive faster," said Morgan.

"We sent out one unit. The rest were with me. They didn't see him."

"Because Rowe is hiding him in Darabee," said Morgan.

"We'll look into that."

Ray knew there was little Jack could do if the neighboring police force was some kind of private army for BEAR. En route Ray told Jack everything he could remember, especially about Rowe's part in giving Morgan's father the access he needed to shoot and kill Sanchez. By the time they reached the station, Jack knew everything Ray did. It made Ray feel better but he also knew he had just put his friend's life at risk. If they were willing to kill him and Morgan on the chance Morgan knew her father's contacts and capture Lisa to ensure Morgan's silence, he had no doubt that Jack's name had just been added to their list of potential threats.

"Be careful," Ray said. "You don't know who they got to."

Jack nodded his understanding and then parked his unit. The minute they cleared the police station doors, Ray was separated from Morgan. Jack stayed with him during the questioning by Agent Forrest and assured him that Chief Tinnin was with Morgan. Ray knew Tinnin was a Turquoise Guardian, but he didn't know him well enough to trust him with Morgan's life.

Kenshaw Little Falcon arrived but Ray was not allowed to see him. Jack was called out to speak to Tinnin and Little Falcon. When he came back he told Ray that Jefferson Rowe was recovering from surgery and expected to make a full recovery. He had engaged an attorney and his room was guarded by both his men and the FBI.

"His attorney is Gaston Wohern," said Jack.

"That supposed to mean something to me?"

"He's out of Phoenix. He is way out of Rowe's league. That means Rowe has friends, the rich kind who hire the best legal counsel money can afford."

"BEAR," said Ray.

Jack nodded. "I'm sure he'll stick to his story that he tried to apprehend Morgan and you and that he was attacked."

"Our word against his," said Ray, knowing whose word would carry more weight.

"We'll keep you here on the rez for now. Best thing."

"You charging me?"

"No, but Rowe will press charges and I'll have to arrest you."

Ray felt afraid for the first time. "You can't. That will leave Morgan unprotected."

"The FBI has the money and they should be preparing a statement to that effect. That should call off all the low-life treasure hunters and opportunists selling her home address and bogus treasure maps."

"But Rowe said that BEAR felt threatened. They're more dangerous than a hundred guys with shovels and dreams of quick money."

"I agree. But I don't know how we can protect her from BEAR."

"We got a look at one of their men. Dylan saw him. The one with the beard." Ray wiped his mouth and thought. "And Rowe. The FBI have to get something out of him. They have to see he's lying."

"You don't have to convince me," said Jack. "You need to convince him." Jack pointed at field agent Luke Forrest. "Because you'll need the Feds' protection to keep Morgan alive."

Chapter Seventeen

Morgan didn't like the deal she'd been offered but she trusted Ray and was beginning to trust Jack. Forrest was another matter. He was too polished and there was a certain hawkish glint to his eyes that made her uncomfortable. Lisa waited with her uncle in the chief's office, but she knew that her uncle was not equipped to protect her daughter.

The FBI was. She glanced from Agent Cosen to Agent Forrest.

"What do I have to do? What exactly?"

They explained it to her. She asked to see Ray and they refused. They would not let her go to Lisa either. But they did promise to release her daughter and her uncle if she didn't agree. That was the deciding factor. She wouldn't let those extremist maniacs at BEAR get to her little girl. And if she had to be human bear bait, then so be it.

"All right. I'll do it."

They had her sign some papers.

In an hour, maybe two, Lisa would be among strangers in protective custody until this was over. But her daughter would be safe. The agents shuffled their papers and excused themselves, leaving her alone with Chief Wallace Tinnin.

She spoke in Tonto Apache, knowing that the agents, now having a private conversation of their own, could not understand.

"I wish Ray could stay with me," she said.

"No, you don't," said the chief.

She understood. To ask Ray to be involved in this was to endanger his life.

"You're right. I don't want him hurt." She just was not going to say why out loud. She might confess to herself that she had fallen in love with Ray Strong. She might even admit that she was aware that Ray was not the kind of man who made commitments to a woman who had a child. But knowing that did not keep her from trying to protect him.

"That's not the reason," said Tinnin.

Morgan wrinkled her brows as unease tugged at the muscles of her shoulders and neck.

"Why then?"

"Because he wasn't sent just to watch over you, Morgan. Kenshaw also sent Ray to find out what you knew about your father's mission."

Her eye rounded. She couldn't breathe. It felt like he had punched her in the stomach.

"No."

Was he one of them, those eco-extremists who had paid her father to murder Sanchez?

The objection sprang from her lips. "He's not one of them."

Tinnin's brow twitched but his face remained somber. "I hope your faith in him isn't misplaced. Strong has a reputation for trouble. He's a wild one. And Kenshaw has ties to some dangerous people. I know that at least one of them is a member of WOLF."

"That's the nonviolent one? The eco-extremists who don't endanger humans."

"Not intentionally, maybe. But driving a nail into a tree when you know a logger will be using a chain saw on it isn't respectful of human life. Soaking a car dealership with gasoline and tossing a match isn't respectful. I believe in protecting the earth, Morgan. But I also believe in protecting humanity."

"Are you telling me that Kenshaw hired Ray to get information on what I know?" said Morgan.

"The FBI agents are speaking to him. Ray asked for me to be present. Detective Bear Den told them that Ray related to him that the head of our medicine society sent Ray to be your protector while he discovered what you knew about your father's business, especially if you knew who hired your father."

"So all this time…" She had trusted him. Confided in him. Slept with him. And just like the other important men in her life, he had deceived her.

RAY DIDN'T LIKE his friend's sour expression. You didn't need to be one of Detective Jack Bear Den's best friends to read his mood from the glowering look and furrowed brow. He had just come from the chief's office where Tinnin and the FBI agents had been questioning Morgan. He could see her through the wall of glass windows but she sat with her back to him.

Ray stood to meet Jack. "Is she all right?"

Jack nodded.

"I want to see her."

Jack's mouth twitched and the breath he drew was long and labored. "But she doesn't want to see you."

"What do you mean?" The fear that he had felt when he'd watched Hatch taken by insurgents came back to gnaw on his gut like termites in wet wood. Before Jack even spoke, he knew because it was the only reason that Morgan would refuse to see him.

Ray sat heavily on his friend's swivel chair staring sightlessly at Jack's desktop. "She knows."

"Tinnin told her about your mission, all of it."

"How did he know?" asked Ray. Ray had confided in only one person and that man was standing right before him. Ray leaped to his feet and grabbed Jack by the front of his shirt. Jack didn't lift a hand.

"You're a Turquoise Guardian!" said Ray. "You're a brother in Tribal Thunder."

Jack's mouth twitched. "I'm also a detective for the tribe."

"You told Tinnin," said Ray.

"Also a Turquoise Warrior. Also my boss and the chief of police."

"Your first responsibility is to your tribe."

Jack shook his head. "It's to the law. And if either you or Kenshaw have broken tribal law, I'm the one who will arrest you."

Ray released him, choosing the reply that would cause the most damage. "You are not Apache."

The hurt filled Jack's face twisting it in an expression of pain mixed with grief.

"Perhaps not. But my heart is Apache." His voice cracked and he swallowed before speaking again. "Do you understand what has happened? These men, the ones that will come next are not after the money. They will come to protect their operation, the operation that has secured an unknown quantity of explosives for an unknown target. They sent Sanchez to kill Amber Kitcheyan not because she realized the mining explosives were missing but because she overheard a name."

"Theron Wrangler," said Ray, knowing Jack's brother Carter had told Jack that before they took him into protective custody.

The implications now settled like dust from the bombshell Jack had just thrown. Morgan had powerful enemies. The kind that hired assassins and arranged mass shootings and stole explosives—all in the name of protecting the earth. But who would protect Morgan?

He would. With everything he had and everything he was. Not only for Kenshaw, his medicine society and for his tribe, but because he needed Morgan to live. No one had to tell him that Morgan deserved better or that he wasn't the sort of man she would choose for a mate and a father to her daughter. But he knew that somewhere along the journey, he had lost his heart to Morgan Hooke.

"Did Kenshaw tell you who hired Morgan's father?"

"You want to read me my rights before you arrest me?" asked Ray.

"I'm not arresting you. I'm asking you a question."

"He did not."

"Do you have knowledge of WOLF, BEAR or the contacts that approached Karl Hooke to hire him to assassinate Sanchez?"

"No, again. I need to speak to her."

Jack shook his head. "She's elected to work with the FBI."

"What? No!"

Ray's gaze flicked to Morgan to find her now watching him with eyes that accused him of deceit.

His friend rested a heavy hand on his shoulder. "Ray, she's traded her cooperation for FBI protection for Lisa."

Ray kept his gaze pinned to Morgan as he spoke to Jack. "*Cooperation*. What does that mean, exactly?"

"It means you're not her protector anymore."

KENSHAW LITTLE FALCON spoke to Cheney Williams on a burner phone. His friend was a well-known environmental attorney and the production manager and long-time confidant for the powerful producer, Theron Wrangler. Williams updated him on Jefferson Rowe's condition.

"He's maintaining his position that he was called in by the tribal police as backup and was the first on the scene. He says that when he tried to place Strong and Hooke under arrest that Ray threw a knife at him."

"The FBI buying that?"

"Not sure. It will be interesting to see who they believe. I'd feel better if Rowe hadn't admitted to

Strong his part in giving Karl Hooke access to his suspect. It lends credence to Strong's story."

"You know what BEAR will do about him?"

"Nothing yet. But they are worried. They are too close to completion to take a risk."

"What about Morgan Hooke and Ray Strong?"

"Strong doesn't know anything but what Rowe told him, which isn't much. But Morgan has seen Rowe with her father. If they believe her and arrest Rowe, then we lose access to Rowe and he can connect the money to our people in WOLF."

"WOLF made the delivery of funds?"

"Yes, to Rowe. Rowe delivered the check to Karl Hooke. Rowe isn't a member of either organization. Wrangler didn't trust him enough. Seems he was right."

"Rowe must know they'll kill him if he talks."

"He's not a fool. He knows they might kill him either way. If I were him, I'd be working out a deal for witness protection."

"How did he know where to look for the money?"

"WOLF's delivery boy recruited him. Wanted Rowe's help to find the money. Now WOLF is on damage control because it's their man who fouled up. BEAR knows that it was WOLF's delivery boy who followed Karl after Rowe delivered the check. Wrangler told me his people didn't know their man went after the cash and had to hear it from him. I don't expect BEAR will forgive the betrayal. His job was delivery and he got greedy."

Kenshaw wished Cheney had given up a name.

"They found it, the money. Morgan and Ray. But hid it again up there in the canyon."

"I'll pass that along."

"Is BEAR going to try to get it back?"

"They don't need money, friend. You know that. They have more money than Turquoise Canyon has water. I'll let you know if I hear whether they'll send someone for Morgan or Rowe."

"Who will they send?"

"That's up to them. Renzo won't make a move without their say-so. They might send his son again."

Kenshaw smiled. He had a name.

Cheney continued. "But his kid already disobeyed orders and they know it. Tough one." There was a pause and Williams cleared his throat. "Kenshaw, your name has come up, too."

"I'm not surprised."

"They know you spoke to the FBI and that you were with Hooke the night he died. Funny. They don't know whether to promote you or kill you."

"Difficult choice."

"You take care. I'll let you know when I hear."

"Walk in beauty, Cheney."

"Many blessings, Kenshaw."

Kenshaw disconnected and handed the phone to FBI agent Forrest.

"Did you get it?"

Chapter Eighteen

Ray waited outside the station for Kenshaw to be released. He knew that finding the money was not enough to protect her. Now he needed to find out who was coming after Morgan. Kenshaw appeared after dark and Ray met him before he reached his truck.

"Ah, there you are. You have done well, Ray," said Kenshaw.

Ray wondered who was right. Jack who said their duty was to the law or their shaman who said their duty was to the tribe. Was Kenshaw using him as a pawn to do the bidding of the eco-extremists?

"She still needs my protection," said Ray.

"Now more than ever. I have called for Tribal Thunder to meet tonight and have a sweat. We will pray and ask for guidance on what we must do."

"Where's Morgan?" asked Ray. "What are they going to do with her?"

"She is still in there." Kenshaw pointed to the station. "And her girl is in protective custody, according to Chief Tinnin. No one but the FBI knows where."

"It's blackmail, using Lisa. She'd do anything to keep her daughter safe," said Ray.

"Any good mother would. The question is can the FBI keep Morgan safe, or do they need the help of Tribal Thunder?"

MORGAN STARED AT the night through tinted glass in the hours when today became tomorrow. Pinyon Forks lay behind her and the community of Koun'nde just ahead. Luke Forrest rode beside her. His partner, Agent Cosen, had preceded them to make arrangements in Morgan's home.

They had allowed her to see Lisa, giving Morgan a chance to explain to her daughter what has happening before her child was moved to a safe house in Phoenix. Lisa was not reassured by strangers, despite the team of agents having included a seemingly very nice Anglo woman. Their parting had been tearful. Morgan's throat still ached along with her head and her heart.

Ray had deceived her, too. Why did this keep happening to her? The worst of it was that she still loved Ray, despite his deception. But she didn't know if she could forgive him.

Field agent Forrest refused her request to remain the night with Lisa, insisting that the less time Morgan spent with the FBI the more likely outsiders were to believe that she was still on the hunt for her father's treasure. Only Morgan's belief that she could not keep her daughter safe gave her the strength to let her go.

Once away, and much to her shame, she admitted to herself that she preferred the lie and Ray's protection to the cold, honest efficiency of the Federal Bureau of Investigations. Was their interest in her any more conscionable than Ray's? They had both wanted something from her, information that she did not have, but could perhaps get. If she didn't die in the process. She thought of Lisa going to live permanently with her mother's brother. Uncle Agustin was a fine man, but too old to raise a girl. Perhaps one of his girls, her cousins, would take Lisa if something happened to her. She knew her tribe would see to raising her daughter but that did not mean she would lie down and die. She planned to fight for survival and her freedom.

Morgan stared at the familiar fence line and the sparse sprinkling of houses. Most were dark because of the late hour and so no one witnessed her return. Still, Forrest explained that her car was waiting close to home and she would drive herself from Koun'nde in case the route was being watched.

"Jefferson Rowe has already had several visitors. We have his room under surveillance, which is why I know that his food tray included a burner phone."

"A what?"

"It's a phone that is very hard to trace. After use, the phone is destroyed."

"Don't you check his tray?"

"Yes, but it was placed on the tray after the nurse carried it past us. She's being questioned, but it looks like she has no involvement other than making a rather poor choice for a payday."

"She'll lose her job."

"Already has," said Forrest.

"I didn't think you would believe me," she said.

Forrest gave her a look. "Not sure we do yet. It seems unlikely that your father, who was so very ill, could have managed to keep all his meetings secret from you. You were his driver, after all."

"I already told you everything I recall."

"Yes." Forrest looked out the window. "Now we need what you don't recall."

They pulled onto a road she knew led only to the upper pasture of one of her neighbors. The headlights showed her battered white Honda. The large SUV drew to a stop.

"We have every room but the bathroom hooked up with video. There are microphones in every room. Just speak to us and we'll hear you."

"How will you know if they are in that extremist group and not just people looking for the money?"

"Because the treasure hunters will be after the money."

He left the rest unsaid. The eco-extremists did not want the blood money they had paid. They wanted the silence that her father had promised. They wanted assurance that his daughter would reveal nothing that could jeopardize their plans. That meant her removal. She knew it. The Feds knew it. That's why they needed her because you couldn't catch a bear without the right kind of bait.

Morgan climbed out of the large SUV used by the FBI and into her shabby wreck. There were a few moments of panic when her car refused to turn over, but at last it gasped to life and she was on her way.

She pulled into her driveway before midnight. The eerie silence of the house stopped her. She gazed up at the starry night and realized that last night at this time she had slept in Ray's embrace and had dreamed of a future that would never be. This morning she had awoken under that same sky and watched the golden sun paint the canyon wall. Now she stood alone before a quiet house that had once held her family.

It was hard not to call a greeting as she entered. The house felt different, empty, invaded, for she knew the agents had been here with their wires and cameras. Some of their essence still remained. She dropped her keys on the counter and slipped out of her coat, draping it on the back of one of the dining room chairs.

There came a scratching from the kitchen door and then a familiar meow. She opened the door to find Cookie looking put out. Lisa's cat! She had forgotten to ask if they had taken Cookie with her daughter. Had the cat walked the several miles from her uncle's home to here? The feline's coat was dusty. Cookie circled her once, rubbing against Morgan's legs and then looking about. Was she searching for Lisa?

"She's not here, Cookie."

The cat regarded her with unblinking eyes.

Morgan scooped up the cat and carried her into the kitchen, crying on her soft, short fur. Cookie tolerated Morgan's weeping to a point and then wriggled until Morgan set her down. Cookie paused at the empty food dish, which Morgan filled before sitting on the floor with her back to the cabinet as Lisa's rescue kitty ate. The smell of the cat food and the sticky noise of Cookie's ingestion made Morgan feel ill and she left Cookie to get ready for bed. When she came back, Cookie stood beside her empty food dish. Morgan changed her water and added dry food to the dish, which Cookie snubbed as she turned to the water instead. Though the house felt empty and she appeared to be alone, she knew the video monitors were all in place, and she wore a wire for when she left her house, plus a tracker to ensure the FBI could locate her or her body.

Cookie demanded egress after her meal and then almost immediately howled for readmission. Once inside she glided past Morgan to Lisa's room where she settled on her daughter's comforter and turned her luminous green eyes on Morgan.

"She won't be back tonight," said Morgan and then thought of the agents listening to her conversing with a cat.

Once in her own bed, she did not sleep, but tossed from side to side, wondering if the microphone was transmitting her heavy sighs and the sound of the toilet flushing. They'd left her no privacy. Agent Cosen had mentioned that she might want to consider a fresh start in witness protection. Such a suggestion showed a complete lack of understanding of who and what she was. You might just as well uproot a pinyon pine and plant it in the Sedona Desert. Her people had fought hard through the federal legal system to gain back their land. She was not leaving her heritage or her daughter's birthright because some crazy group was trying to return the southwest to its natural state.

Morgan closed her eyes, kicked at the covers,

rolled and finally forced herself to stillness. Now only her mind raced. Finally she left her bed in favor of Lisa's. There, with Cookie coiled at her feet, Morgan finally dozed.

She woke when the duct tape blanketed her mouth.

Chapter Nineteen

Morgan's eyes opened to darkness as cold hands seized her. She writhed, struggling to escape, the duct tape muffling her cries. Something pricked her neck. The injection took her quickly as her mind clawed to remain conscious but her body felt strangely detached as if wrapped in cotton.

The covers fell back and rough hands pushed up her tank top. The cool air brushed her bare skin. A dark shape loomed over her. She tried to scream. The adhesive of the tape tugged at her mouth. The intruder's gloved hands brushed down her sternum and swept along in the darkness down her hip, over her legs but the touch felt a long way off somehow, as if her skin no longer wholly belonged to her.

She could feel herself sliding away. Her eyes slid closed against her command as her hammering heart slowed and she accepted that she would die.

Ray.
Lisa.
She closed her eyes and fought to stay alive.

RAY BREATHED IN the sweet moist air inside the sweat lodge. He sat in his black cotton gym shorts wearing nothing but his medicine bundle. The other men sat in a circle around the fire pit of hot river stones prepared in the sacred fire that sat outside the wickiup beyond the entrance that stood in the eastern portion of the round, domed enclosure.

Whether by design or unintentionally, they had left two places empty. One had belonged to Hatch Yeager, their fallen comrade. The second had recently been vacated by Carter Bear Den.

Outside the sun would soon break the line of mountains to the east, but inside was as dark as the burrow of a rabbit. The three remaining members of Tribal Thunder, Ray Strong, Dylan Tehauno and Jack Bear Den, listened as their shaman spoke of the need to replace Carter Bear Den. Jack was opposed, insisting that his brother would return, but Kenshaw said the group was out of balance with only three. Four was the sacred number in the medicine wheel because there were four directions, four seasons, four stages of a man's life and four characteristics of a warrior. Many things in the world moved in a circle. Jack's objections were assuaged when Kenshaw suggested the inclusion of his younger brother Kurt, now twenty-four and a paramedic for the air ambulance out of Darabee.

With that settled, Kenshaw turned to the matter of Morgan Hooke, now under the protection of the FBI.

"You are no longer responsible for this one," said Kenshaw to Ray. "She has chosen another protector. Your mission now is to help Jack and Dylan protect our land and our tribe."

But Ray still felt responsible for Morgan and Lisa, more now than before. He knew that the moment they had finished their business and prayed their prayers, he would return to watch over her.

The matter of the stabbing of Chief Jefferson Rowe was still under investigation. He now shared Jack's suspicions regarding their shaman's connection to the eco-extremists. But Jack cared about upholding the law and Ray cared about protecting Morgan. Kenshaw's foreknowledge of the attack at the Lilac Mine and the steps he had taken to protect Morgan and Lisa could not be consigned to intuition. Despite their uncertainties, both were respectful of the sweat lodge. This sacred ritual would not be sullied with accusations.

Kenshaw poured water on the hot coals, sending steam through the green cedar boughs. Ray breathed deep and joined in the chanting prayer.

The men were a unit of brothers, but now doubt had come into their midst and Ray felt the distrust as strongly as he felt the sweat running in rivulets down his nearly naked body. He looked at the empty place where his best friend should be and for an instant before he blinked his eyes, he thought he saw Hatch sitting among them. Ray stared but there was nothing there. It did not matter, because now every hair on his body stood up.

Ray pointed to the place and told the others what he had seen. There was much said of ghosts in Apache culture and most of it very bad. His ancestors went to great lengths to see that ghosts did not return to this world and Ray could not keep the dread from filling his chest.

"A warning," said Kenshaw. "Something unseen."

"It's a flashback," said Jack. "I get them sometimes, too."

Ray looked at him. Jack had never told him that. In fact they never spoke of the night Hatch was taken.

"Me, too," said Dylan.

Ray's skin itched and the sweat stung his eyes. "Something is wrong. I have to go."

Kenshaw nodded. "It is time for all of us to greet the day with a prayer and blessing."

Their shaman ducked out of the wickiup and into the cool, crisp morning air. Jack followed and then Dylan. They each took a turn sluicing water from the stream over their heads with a bucket. The icy water puckered his skin and washed away the sweat until he felt clean and alive. Soon they were shivering in their gym shorts, which they discarded to tug on dry clothing.

Kenshaw finished last, seeing that the sacred fire was out. When he finished they sat in a circle by the stream. Dylan, their drum keeper, set out the large barrel that had once been a portion of a ponderosa pine, hollowed now and with a cowhide stretched tight over the gap. They used bowed willow sticks to communally strike the rhythm. Kenshaw sang in a high true modulation encouraging many blessings for their people, and the three members of Tribal Thunder repeated the last portion of his prayer together in one voice. This, too, was a vital role of the medicine society, to follow the path walked by those who came before and mark the way for those who would follow.

The sun peeked over the ridge, sending bright beams of golden light across the land. Still Ray found no peace but battled the continuing feeling that he was not where he was supposed to be.

Was she sleeping in her bed or did the FBI have her in some hotel room under guard? Would he be able to see her? Now that she knew of his duplicity, would she even want to see him?

He did not expect her forgiveness but he lived

in hope that he could earn a second chance because Morgan's happiness was nearly as dear to him as her safety. Ray prayed louder as the sun's apex crested the trees. Behind them, the hillside flooded with light.

Please keep her safe, Ray thought.

Jack seemed impatient to finish and was on his feet before the drum had gone silent.

Now the detective reemerged as he asked Kenshaw the questions he had held back during the sacred time inside the wickiup and here in the drum circle.

"How do you know the plans of these extremist groups?"

"Extremist." Kenshaw laughed. "There was a time when the Tonto people were extremists. Enemies to be eliminated."

"Are you one of them?" asked Jack.

"I have been many things in my life," said Kenshaw. "I have taken part in acts of civil disobedience for causes I believe are right. To stop wars. To take back land and water rights. To keep peace with other nations and to protect the earth that is our home. Yes, I am a part of all things as are you."

"How do you know these things before anyone else?" asked Ray.

Kenshaw smiled. "I have lived a long time. I hear things on the wind and from cellular tow-ers." He laughed. "But if you ask me to tell you who speaks to me, I will say what I said to Agent Forrest. It is my right to speak and it is my right to be silent."

"Are you one of them? Of those eco-extremists that call themselves BEAR?"

"I am not."

Jack seemed relieved, but Ray noticed their shaman did not deny membership in WOLF.

"WOLF?" asked Ray.

"If I answer that, my friend Jack here will have to arrest me."

Jack seemed ready to arrest him anyway but was interrupted by the chiming of his phone, which sounded at the same moment as Kenshaw's and Ray's. They lifted their mobiles. The text was from Luke Forrest and was only three words: Important—call me.

The chill Ray had experienced in the sweat lodge and the vision of his fallen friend now pressed on him. He knew before he was told that something terrible was happening. He issued a prayer as he called Forrest and pressed the speaker button.

"Is it Morgan?" asked Ray.

"Yes. We've lost contact." He told Ray that they had last seen her a little after one in the morning and only with the daylight realized that her bedroom was empty and Morgan gone.

"Did she slip away?" asked Jack. "Or evade your custody?"

"That's the question. We know that Dylan and Ray have tracking experience. We'd like their opinion."

Ray was already running toward his vehicle. The fifteen miles to Morgan's home were the longest of his life. They reached the small home and he and Dylan went to work, conferring as they checked first inside and then outside and came to the same conclusion. Ray took off on the trail, moving carefully. He heard Dylan speaking to Forrest and Cosen.

"She was taken by force out that window," said Dylan.

Ray headed toward Guy Heron's home and tried to keep the rage from consuming him.

"One man," said Ray, his words still clear. "When he left, he was carrying Morgan."

"How do you know that?" asked Agent Cosen.

"Depth of the footprints compared to entry," said Ray. "And nothing else is missing that would weigh enough to account for the difference."

Forrest trailed Ray. He glanced back at his shadow.

"My grandfather had a reputation for tracking," said Forrest. "I was lucky to have known him and to have learned some of what he knew."

Ray pointed at the exposed stretch of sand and the footprints. "What do you see?"

"He has a head start, judging from the sand that has fallen into the tracks. He is wearing boots and, guessing from the size, he's male."

Ray nodded. "And Morgan did not shift her weight as they carried her. These prints are straight and the tread natural."

Forrest met his gaze but did not seem to understand.

"She wasn't moving," said Ray.

Forrest's eyes widened. "But no blood."

That was true. Ray hoped that Morgan was alive.

"You can't get information from a dead woman, at least not the kind that will tell them where to find the treasure."

But killing someone was an excellent way to be sure that no one else got information from them. Ray moved more quickly now.

He had to find her before it was too late.

Chapter Twenty

Morgan woke by slow degrees. First to the pain of her legs, cramped and alive with pins and needles. Next she recognized from the groan that tried to escape her that her mouth had been taped. With her eyes now opened, she found her vision clear but she could see nothing from under the camouflage-patterned vinyl tarp that covered her. The motor sound and the jostling alerted her to movement. Her best guess was that she rode in a cart fixed to a four-wheeler of some sort and that they were on an incline. It didn't take a genius to deduce why someone would steal her from her bed and drag her up a mountain. The trouble was the money was no longer here. Likely her captors would not know that because the FBI had not revealed that the money had been recovered. Instead, they told her, they let word out that she and Ray had admitted to finding the treasure and hiding it again before they were taken into custody.

Her abductor must want the treasure or she would already be dead. The trick would be to lead them to a treasure that was no longer here and stay alive until help arrived.

She was so grateful that her daughter was safely away. But how had her abductor managed to grab her right out from under the FBI surveillance? Or perhaps the FBI had let him take her. Were they following them? Either way, the sun was well up judging from the light through the tarp and the heat that made her entire body damp with sweat. She was so thirsty. The need for water tormented her far more than the pain in her hip and the tingling in her legs. Now she had to figure out how to stay alive until help reached her.

Ray. She spoke to him in her mind. Apologizing for leaving him without thanks. He had not told her everything, but he had kept his word, protecting her and helping her retrieve the money. Once they found it, many men would have just helped themselves. Ray had not done that.

Of course it was logical to assume that her father had told her everything. But her father was wiser than that. He'd tried to find a way to protect her from the men who had hired him while still giving her the money. Hadn't he known her well enough to understand that she would never keep it?

Would Ray come after her or, with his mission complete, would he leave her to the wolves?

The cart hit a particularly vicious rock, sending her airborne for just a minute before throwing her back down to collide with the metal floor. The jolt got her moving, searching beneath the tarp for something she could use as a weapon or to cut the ties that secured her wrists behind her.

The forward motion stopped, sending her skidding along the floor. The motor cut and Morgan held her breath. Should she be unconscious or try to spring at him? Even if she managed to knock him down, would she have time to find something to cut her ties and run?

An instant later the tarp fell back and the brilliant sunlight poured down on her. She managed to look far woozier than she was as her kidnapper lowered the rear gate. He wore camo from his hood to his boots. Across his face he had a camouflage mask, likely designed to make him invisible to prey. Today it served to make him a faceless menace that froze her blood on this hot morning. Was it good that she couldn't identify him?

Perhaps.

She looked about for another attacker but found them alone.

Her captor tugged her out the back of the cart. She did not have to pretend that her legs would not support her and went down so fast he could only slow her descent. He swore and then retrieved a knife from his belt then cut the plastic at her ankles.

"Get up."

She didn't. Instead she sprawled on her stomach, hoping he'd cut the bonds at her wrists. But he used those bonds to tug her to a sitting position.

"Up!"

Morgan complied, but she had managed to rub her face over the sandstone. The tape across her mouth was now curled at one side.

"I know the others didn't find it," he said. He sounded Anglo to her and young. "I'm betting you did. Our man said he could be trusted. But then he goes off with you and finds it."

Ray, he was speaking of Ray. But why would this man think that Ray could be trusted? And who was their man?

"That's right. Your boyfriend was working for us all along. You really think we'd leave you for the FBI to question without knowing what your dad told you?"

Oh, no. That couldn't be. Ray had told her he was assigned by the Turquoise Guardians. Had that also been a lie?

Her captor grabbed her arm in a punishing grip. "You're going to show me where you hid it. No sense in leaving it out here to rot."

Morgan struggled to speak, making a series of muffled sounds.

"You don't need to talk to show me where it is. So get moving." He gave her a shove.

She staggered forward and then looked around. They were at the base of the upper ruins. She was staring right at the spiraling symbol marking the winter solstice. The sun had already reached the canyon floor and the shadow rock now served no purpose. Morgan thought. A plan came to her that was followed immediately by thoughts of all the ways it could go wrong.

But she had nothing better so she walked to the notched log that served as a ladder and she lifted her gaze to the upper ruins.

"I knew it. I was sure because he had me wait down past the turn. I followed your dad after I delivered the check to Rowe and again when he cashed it the next day. He drove down here in that heap of a pickup with the four wheeler in the back, but he was so quick and I was on foot."

Delivered the check? He was one of them, the eco-extremists.

"You're wondering why I didn't just take it from him before he drove up here, right?"

She hadn't gotten to that yet.

"Because he hadn't done the job yet. But really. What does a dead man need with all that money? Can't spend it."

He was one of them. A WOLF or a BEAR. She wanted to ask him what they were going to do with the explosives, the target, the FBI called it. But her mouth was taped shut.

So her father had come here with this man in tow, tapped out the clue in the chimney and they'd driven up here to bury the money at the base of the cliff.

Morgan put her foot on the notched log that lay at the base of the cliff.

"Okay. I gotcha." He lifted the ladder and propped it against the rock face. "Ladies first."

Was he kidding? She couldn't climb with her hands bound. Morgan turned her back and lifted her clasped wrists.

"Just so you know, I hid the only key to the four-wheeler and I'm packing heat. You try anything and you'll be bleeding all over this canyon."

She nodded her head in understanding, waiting. Next came the scrape of the knife leaving the sheath. He wouldn't kill her yet because he needed her to find the treasure but still her breath caught and held. He inserted the blade between her hands and tugged. The bonds fell away and she extended her cramped fingers, then rolled her wrists as the breath she held escaped into the dry air.

"Let's go," he growled.

Morgan marched to the ladder like a good little soldier, tugging at the gray duct tape as she went.

Her skin tingled where the adhesive had clung. She was an excellent climber. And she needed to make the climb of her life now. Morgan placed a hand on the notch at eye level and mentally prepared herself. A rush of adrenalin flooded through her bloodstream making her heart pound and her ears buzz. But she held herself back, beginning the climb with a slow and careful focus. Then she felt the ladder shift, as he joined her on the climb. That instant Morgan took off, climbing with a speed that bordered on recklessness.

"Hey! Slow down."

She didn't of course, because she knew that he could not hold the ladder and a pistol. This would be her only chance. The people here before her knew something about defending against their enemies and he had inadvertently sent her to a stronghold perfect for defense.

Morgan reached the top of the ladder and used the niches carved in stone to scramble the last few feet up and over the ledge and onto the wide, flat plateau that formed the cavern floor. She did not pause as she ran to the forked branch resting inside the first room of the honeycomb of apartments. She would have only one chance at this. She dragged the branch behind her as she hurried to the edge.

Morgan threw herself to her stomach and extended the branch over the edge. Her kidnapper was already reaching for the niches in the stone.

"Hey. Don't!"

But she did, catching the top of the log in the notch and pushing. He made a desperate choice then, releasing the niche to scramble downward. Had he chosen to lurch upward he might have reached her. Instead he slid down the log as if it were an enormous fireman's pole. As a result, he was midway down the forty-foot log at something between a fall and a slide when she dislodged the ladder. It toppled with him still clinging to it like an ant on a blade of grass. She had to admire how he was able to get his feet under him and pushed off so that he was falling free and clear of the giant ponderosa trunk for the last ten feet. His landing was hard and simultaneous with the log. The dust rose but she could see him, sprawled on the loose shale and rock. He didn't move.

She took the opportunity to gather several stones from the broken wall, ignoring the thirst that had turned her tongue to sandpaper.

She knew her history. Knew that the upper ruins were known by outsiders as Apache Leap, the stronghold that none could find during the Apache Wars. But the Apache Scouts had discovered her people and brought the cavalry. General Crook had hurled boulders down on her ancestors. There was no room in the cavern for all of them. Caught between the falling stones and the cliff, many of the men, women and children had chosen to leap to their deaths.

Morgan dropped one stone from the wall at the edge of the cavern floor and then another. She checked. Her captor was not moving. Morgan briefly considered throwing them down on the fallen man, but she did not have the stomach for it. Such things marked the soul.

Instead she sat back to wait. The FBI might not know where she was, but Ray and Jack and Dylan would find her. She had confidence in Tribal Thunder. Were they on their way now?

She peered over the edge at the still form and prayed they would come soon.

Morgan missed Ray. True, she had faulted him for doing as his medicine society had asked him. What had he done to her really? Had it been a lie or had he just kept his secrets? She thought of Lisa's father who had deceived her and of how she had never told a soul about him, not even her father, until she had spoken the truth to Ray. But all those years she had kept silent. Wasn't she entitled to her secrets? Wasn't he?

He had been assigned to her protection. He had also been given an objective. And although she had been an assignment at first, she believed all that had changed the night they had slept here in this canyon. At least it had changed for her because against all her best judgment and her past experience, she had fallen in love with Ray. And she planned to tell him so. Now all she had to do was stay alive up here on the hot stone beneath the blazing sun with no water until he arrived.

Chapter Twenty-One

Ray and Dylan agreed on the tracks and followed them to the driveway of a neighbor. Chief Tinnin and FBI rousted the occupants but they had seen and heard nothing.

"We let it out that Morgan found the money and left it up in the canyon by the upper ruin," said field agent Cassidy Cosen.

Ray did not need any more information. He was already running for his truck.

"Wait," said Forrest. "We're getting four-wheelers from Tucson."

How long would that take? The machines were faster, but Ray had a trailer and two good horses that loaded well. Dylan swung up into the passenger side.

"We'll meet them," said Dylan.

It seemed to take forever to load the gear, horses and supplies. But both men knew better than to go into the canyon unprepared. The drive along

Turquoise Lake to the lower ruins was only seven miles but it was insufferable to Ray who cursed at every slow-moving truck and each winding turn.

"It's not faster if you put us in a ditch," said Dylan.

Ray gritted his teeth and hunched over the wheel as they bumped into the lot and saw the sign that announced a permit was required to visit the ruins. Permits were necessary for outsiders, not members of their tribe. The lone blue pickup parked here did not display a permit but did have a residential parking permit for Phoenix affixed to its front windshield.

Ray pulled in beside the vehicle and threw his truck into Park and Dylan exhaled loudly as he released his hold on the overhead hand grip. They left the truck and met again behind the trailer. Ray swung the rear gate open.

"Look at that!" Dylan pointed skyward.

Ray glanced up and was rewarded by the sight of a canary-yellow hot-air balloon floating up and over Turquoise Lake.

"Is that today?" Dylan asked, referring to the semiannual hot-air balloon festival that began and ended off tribal lands but drifted over their airspace.

Ray had no time for hot air. The air down here was hot enough and he knew what this kind of heat could do to a person. Did she have water? He backed out the first mount, a gray gelding. Dylan followed a moment later with the chestnut with white stockings. They swung the blankets and saddles up in unison.

"You think about that Indian Relay Race at all?" asked Dylan.

Ray grunted and cinched the girth so tight the gelding groaned. He let the strap out a notch.

"'Cause I don't think those Brule Sioux have anything on Apache when it comes to horse racing."

Ray shook his head and loaded the water and pack on his mount. Next he checked his rifle and then slid it into the sheath and tied it to the D-ring on the front of the saddle. Finally, he swung up. They were off. After the lower ruins the trail wound up giving him glimpses of the dirt lot below. The outsider's vehicle and his truck and trailer were still the only vehicles parked there. If the FBI were coming, they certainly were taking their time. Ray looked forward now. He and Dylan were on their own. The trick would be to find Morgan and her kidnapper before he knew that they were there.

His ancestors had a fierce reputation as warriors. He and Dylan and Carter and Jack and Hatch were warriors, if modern ones. He was well trained and ready for a fight. But he'd never faced a foe with so much fear in his heart. If anything happened to Morgan, he would never forgive himself. He had to reach her soon. He had to bring her home to Lisa. Ray swallowed at the lump rising in his throat as he realized the terrible truth.

Somewhere along the way, he'd ceased to follow his shaman's orders and begun to follow the whispering of his heart. He loved her but with the dry air and relentless sun that might not be enough to keep her alive.

MORGAN SQUINTED AGAINST the harsh sunlight. The urge to move to the shade and relative cool of the cave lured but to do so was to lose sight of her captor. Unfortunately, to remain here at the rim in the rising heat of the day threatened her in other ways. She scanned the canyon floor for rescue but, seeing none, she despaired. The unrelenting heat of the rock rim at midday stole her strength, killing her bit by bit. Her head pounded and her tongue stuck to the roof of her dry mouth. Her pulse was too fast and she now struggled with dizziness. She tried to recall the last water she had tasted. Last night, a small swallow after brushing her teeth. If only she had known.

Morgan forced herself up and to the lip of the cave, where she discovered that the man was not only up but he was also heading to the four-wheeler and retrieving a rifle. If he intended to shoot her out of her cave, he had better have something more than a .38. He lifted the rifle stock to his shoulder and she drew back from the edge.

A moment later bullets pinged off the rock, peppered with some very colorful language. She did not reply to the barrage of bullets or foul names. She did move to the far side of the ledge, affording her a different view and the chance to see him before he spotted her. The man was up on his feet. He had removed the camouflage head cover and looked up at the place where the ladder had rested. She stared at the unfamiliar face. As she suspected from his speech, he was Anglo. His hair was light brown and short, his face fleshy with a jawline obscured in a double chin both of which were in need of a shave. Blood flowed in a steady stream from his cheek. His hands bled, likely from his rapid descent down the log and his clothing was coated in dust.

She did not want to hurt him but she also did not want to die of dehydration up on this ledge. She eyed the orange cooler strapped to the cart behind his four-wheeler. Then she searched down the canyon for any sign of rescue. Was Ray in one of those shiny beetle bright vehicles winding along the ribbon of road that threaded around Turquoise Lake?

Something above her caught her attention. Big and bright and yellow as a summer squash and rising in the blue sky. It was a balloon, the kind they launched for tourists from Goodwin Lake. Another appeared over the ridge of the canyon wall, this one had wide blue-and-red vertical stripes. When the rainbow balloon appeared she recalled the hot-air-balloon festival that took place each April. She and her father used to sit on the back porch and watch them float by. They could even hear the sound of the fire from the tanks that lifted the voluminous nylon up into the sky.

The sound of shoed horses brought her attention rapidly back to earth. But the source of it did not make sense. Beyond this canyon lay miles of Mazatzal Mountains and no easy access to roads or trails. A person would have to ride up the parallel canyon and then circle back to reach this place from the northwest. Morgan pushed up and away from the lip of the canyon to get a better look at the riders. Hope rose but she knew that most of the tribe's horses were not shod and she could clearly hear the steady clank of horseshoes on stone.

Her abductor must have heard it as well because he lowered his rifle to listen and then swung the weapon toward the two men who rode in line with a pack horse on a lead following behind.

One rode a large chestnut and the other a piebald with a white rump and black tail. The pack animal was a lathered dun with a head hanging from fatigue. The riders seemed easy in the saddle, dressed in jeans, boots and long sleeved shirts. Their riding gloves and the broad cowboy hats made it impossible for her to determine their ethnicity or anything other than that they were of average build and both carried rifles, sheathed and tied to their saddles.

"Gifford, you damned fool. You took off your mask?"

She judged the speaker to be the lead rider. His words had an odd quality. Not muffled exactly but vibrating in a way that did not seem quite natural.

Her abductor lowered his rifle and took two steps backward as if struck.

"Bleeding all over himself, too," said the second rider, coming abreast of the first.

"I—I..." Gifford did not make a winning reply.

"Where is she?"

Gifford pointed and Morgan tensed. She did not draw back from the lip but continued to stare down. The first man glanced up at her and then the second. She frowned as she tried to make sense of what she saw. They wore masks, the molded plastic kind. The first man wore a red fox mask and the second the likeness of a brown bear. A chill slithered up her spine.

"What did you tell her?"

"Nothin'. I swear. I just said she was going to take me to the money."

"What were your orders?" said Mr. Fox.

"Deliver the check to Rowe and return to base," said Gifford. His voice had taken on a tone of contrition showing weakness and submission. "I did that."

"You returned two days late," said Mr. Bear. "And now you're back up here."

Gifford's head hung and he did not meet the gaze of the animal spirit men that questioned him. "But she hid the money up here. I was going to get it back for us. For the cause."

Even from here, Morgan could smell the lie. Gifford had been acting for Gifford and now he was facing his superiors and the music.

"It's not our money. It was payment for a job that was completed," said Mr. Bear, glancing up at her.

Morgan shifted, trying to resist the urge to disappear from their sight.

"Your father wanted you to have that money, Morgan, you and your young daughter, Lisa."

She scowled, hating that they knew her name and the name of her daughter. The tiny hairs lifted on her body and for an instant, the blazing heat of the sun and the broiler that the flat rock beneath her had become were forgotten, as her skin went cold. It was a threat and she recognized it as such.

"Are you the ones who tried to take my daughter?" Her voice sounded strange, hoarse and scratchy.

The bear shook his head. "Not ours. Treasure hunter out of Tucson."

"But she has the money. It's up here," whined Gifford.

"But she doesn't. Kenshaw thinks she does. Not me. She's too honest. If she weren't, the Feds would still have her in custody. She cut a deal, sure as I live." Mr. Bear looked up at her through the two circular holes in his plastic mask. "You gave it all to the Feds. Didn't you? I would think a Tonto woman would have more sense than to trust the descendants of the men who stood on this cliff and hurled rocks down on your women and children." The man lowered his head, returning his attention to Gifford as he drew his rifle and rested the stock on his thigh.

"She didn't give it back. It's here," said Gifford.

"That's what they wanted you to believe," said Mr. Fox. "It's a lie and a lure and you swallowed it whole. I don't expect you to think for yourself— I expect you to follow orders. Did that oath you swore to our brothers in WOLF mean nothing?"

Was she looking down at two members of the extremists' branch of BEAR? Morgan began to tremble. Forrest had told her that these men made no effort to preserve human life in their quest to return the land to its natural state. They had the mining explosives and they had the only man who could identify them, one from among their own ranks, killed by her father's bullet.

"I'm sorry, Mr…" Gifford paused in mid-sentence as the man in the bear mask aimed his rifle at Gifford's head.

Gifford raised his hands in a gesture of surrender and defense. But flesh and bone is no shield against a bullet. The man in the bear mask fired. Morgan gave an involuntary shout as Gifford fell to his knees and then sprawled forward in the sand.

"Check him," said Mr. Bear, still aiming his rifle at the motionless, prone figure.

From her vantage point the scene seemed surreal, the effect amplified by being light-headed. Morgan's heart beat very fast but whether from the shock or from the unrelenting heat, she did not know. She gazed down on the smaller figures as the fox dismounted and checked for a pulse on Gifford's neck, kneeling, waiting and then shaking his head.

"Got him," said Mr. Fox.

"Greedy fool," said Mr. Bear as he sheathed his rifle. "He was about to say my name. They'll be questioning his father now. Have to cut him loose for a while. See if he's really one of us now."

Morgan imagined someone hurting Lisa. She would never give her allegiance to such a man.

Mr. Bear's gaze went to Morgan. She glanced toward the stack of rocks she'd collected. "Hot day, today, Ms. Hooke. I figure you have a few hours at best. If help comes in that time, you might survive. I do not plan to kill you because my sources say you do not know me or any of my compatriots."

She tried to speak but her tongue felt clumsy and thick in her mouth. Her spit was like paste. She cleared her raw throat and exhaled, knowing the dry air stole water from her lungs with each breath. She needed drink and the sight of the water strapped to the men's saddles tortured her.

"I don't know you," she said, her voice a rasp.

"Did your father name us?"

"No."

"He was a smart man and we owe him a debt. I'm sorry for your loss. You can take comfort in the knowledge that your father died for a great cause."

Her father died in a vain attempt to earn enough money to support her and Lisa when she would have given it all back again to spend just five more minutes with him.

"Time to go," said the fox.

The buzzing in her ears grew louder. Morgan looked down at the two men in plastic masks and smiled. Why did their smiling faces and long snouts seem so funny?

Her head pounded and she just wanted to rest and drink water and ice tea and pink lemonade.

In her confusion, she almost crawled headfirst off the cliff. She was also slow to recognize that the sound she heard was not in her head but coming from down the canyon. A motor.

Mr. Fox mounted up.

"Farewell, Morgan Hooke," called Mr. Bear, touching the brim of his hat. "I wonder if you will be alive to greet your friends. Nature is a harsh taskmaster."

Then the two men turned their horses and retreated back up the canyon.

"That's the wrong way," she whispered, knowing they'd be trapped up there. That meant the FBI and possibly Tribal Thunder would have to face these two faceless men in masks. She didn't want that.

Ray. She had to warn him to keep him away from Mr. Fox and Mr. Bear.

Chapter Twenty-Two

The sound of the shot brought Ray to a halt. He rose in his stirrups to look up the trail but he could see nothing. They had stopped only once, to let the horses drink.

He glanced back to see Dylan looking up the canyon. He met Ray's gaze and nodded.

Ray pressed his heels into his gelding's sides and shot forward. He had the rifle out, gripping the stock as he guided his mount up the steep grade. They were only a few hundred yards from the ruins and Ray knew in his pounding heart that Morgan was there. Hope and dread blended like blood in water as he raced forward, praying and cursing in turns.

He barreled around the curve of the steep canyon wall as another hot-air balloon drifted over the gap in the stone above. Finally he sighted the cave and the ruins. An instant later he saw the still form lying at the base of the cliff. He pulled up on the reins as his heart seemed to rise into his throat, choking him and blurring his vision. Was it Morgan?

He urged his horse forward, the hoof beats landing with the rhythm of his heart. A man lay motionless in the sand, sprawled as if he had fallen from the upper ruins. Ray's head sank in relief as he recognized it was not Morgan.

Behind him, Ray heard the click of a cocking rifle. He glanced forward and saw two mounted men. One aimed his weapon at Dylan, the other aimed at Ray. Their wide-brimmed hats shaded their faces but it seemed that they wore some grotesque, grinning animal masks. He glanced from one to the other, looking for Morgan.

Where was she?

"Mr. Strong. Mr. Tehauno," called one. "You are early."

"Where's Morgan?" shouted Ray. He gripped his weapon but did not raise it. Ray nudged his horse forward. "What have you done with her?"

"Nothing but stay out of range of her rocks." He pointed up to the cliff dwelling.

Ray saw an arm dangling over the ledge. He watched and saw no movement. He turned back to the men. "What's wrong with her?"

"Carelessness. Mr. Journey no doubt failed to see her properly hydrated. She was red faced when we arrived but I see now she has gone pale."

Dylan spoke up now. "If you've harmed her—"

"The heat has done that." The man in the mask of the bear turned to look through small circular eye holes at Ray. "So you have a choice. You can try and stop us or you can save yon maiden in her tower from the fiery sun dragon."

Ray sheathed his rifle. Then he was off his horse and running for the ladder cut from the pine trunk, water bottle in his hand. Dylan kept his rifle aimed as the two men set their mounts in motion. By the time Dylan joined him, Ray could see the two weaving up the steep grade that he knew led deeper into the box canyon.

"They'll be trapped up there," said Dylan.

The two men rode out of range as Ray reached the top of the ladder. There was a time when he might have thought twice about choosing not to stand his ground. But that was before a certain Apache woman had burrowed into his heart.

When he crested the top, holding the strap of the water bottle in his teeth, he found Morgan lying on her belly with her cheek on the hot stone cave floor. She wore a dirty powder-blue tank top and boy shorts that hugged her hips. Her legs sprawled out as if she had been bracing as she looked over the edge. Beside her was a pile of stones she had likely removed from the masonry of the dwelling walls for defense against the attack from below.

"Morgan!" She did not move or give any sign that she heard his cry.

He sank to his knees beside her and gripped her arm, finding it slack and hot. He rolled her limp form up off the hot stone and onto his lap. Her eyelids fluttered but her eyes rolled back in her head showing the whites. His panic swelled as he struggled to unscrew the wide black cap from the water bottle.

"Dylan! Bring all the water you can carry up here."

His friend shouted an affirmation.

Ray's hands trembled as he poured water over her head and ruffled her hair to be sure the water soaked her boiling head. Then he doused her shirt. Still she didn't move. He stripped out of his shirt, leaving him in only his straw cowboy hat, jeans and boots. He soaked his shirt and laid it across her forehead, soaking her hair. Then he lifted her and ran her back into the recesses of the cliff dwelling. How had she gotten away?

Her shirt was already dry. He soaked it again and then soaked her shorts. Her face remained an unnatural gray. He checked her pulse and his panic rose when he found her heart beat as fast as a captured bird's.

At the time of her birth Morgan would have been given a bead carved from an abalone shell. All Apache girls received such a bead, just as the boys received a similar one fashioned of turquoise. At the time of their death they would fly through the hole in the bead and to the world of spirits in less time than it took to blink an eye. Ray kept his bead in his medicine bundle. He did not know where a woman kept her bead, but he hoped it was now far, far away. He prayed aloud in the language of his ancestors for Morgan to linger here with him on earth. He made her promises that he knew she would not want him to keep, promises for a future together with a man who did not deserve her but loved her with his whole heart.

Dylan appeared wearing his saddlebags like a backpack and with a coil of rope over one arm.

"She's too hot," said Ray.

Dylan checked her by touching the back of his hand to Morgan's cheek. "We have to get her off this ledge."

"Cool her first. Take off your shirt. Soak it and put it on her legs." Together they continued to douse her with water. Her eyes fluttered but she did not rouse.

Dylan looked at Ray with an expression of a man who has not given up hope but is considering it.

"Dylan, I can't lose her, too."

His friend sucked in a breath. But if anyone could understand, it was Dylan. His friend knew Ray had lost his parents and his best friend. And by saying, too, Ray had lifted Morgan into the circle of those closest and most dear to his heart. Dylan's brow furrowed and he nodded.

"Soak her again," said Dylan.

"It's my fault," said Ray. "Just like the last time."

"That wasn't your fault. Neither is this."

Ray shook his head, feeling the moisture well in his eyes and knowing Morgan's poor little body was too hot and too dry to even cry. "If I hadn't deceived her, she wouldn't have gone to the FBI. I would have been there when that creep came for her."

"We got her, Ray. We'll get her down and get her evac'd out."

"If she dies…" He couldn't say it because he didn't know what he would do. What Lisa would do. He pressed one hand to his forehead and wept. "I love her. That's why she's going. Everyone I love…"

Dylan had him by the wrist and gave a jolting tug. Ray glanced at him. "We need to get her down. They'll be here any minute. They have the four-wheelers. But we have to move."

Ray stood, carrying Morgan in his arms.

"Too dangerous to climb. We need to lower her down." Dylan released the ties that held the bedroll from his back. They wrapped Morgan and soaked her and the blanket with the last of the water. Then they tied the rope around her. Ray stood back to brace himself as he wrapped the rope around his back. Dylan eased Morgan over the edge and gradually released the rope, allowing Ray to take her weight. Ray kept the rope around his back and used one gloved hand to slow Morgan's descent by pressing the rope down and around the inside of his thigh. Gradually he let the rope slide through his hands. Dylan called out her progress. When he slid halfway down, Ray pictured Morgan there, wrapped in a brightly colored Pendleton blanket, twisting between heaven and earth. It was a good place for a soul to slip free and that thought made him want to hurry her down, but he forced himself to go slowly, letting the rope go inch by inch.

"I'm going down. I'll tug when I have her." Dylan disappeared over the edge leaving him with his fears and the diminishing coil of rope.

He looked at the unforgiving sky and watched the hot-air balloons floating peacefully past on the currents of hot air. He could even see some of their passengers looking down at the life-and-death struggle visible beneath their baskets. Then he looked higher. There above the tops of a colorful collection of balloons and beneath the burning sun soared an eagle. Where once the eagle had helped him see far and true. Now all he could see was Morgan's hot face and his dreams of a future with her floating away on the currents of hot air.

Chapter Twenty-Three

Ray felt the tug on the rope that told him Morgan was safely in Dylan's arms. He eased off the tension and then moved to the edge to look to the canyon floor.

"She's hot again. And her clothing is already dry."

They needed to get her back to the spring some three hundred yards down the canyon. Ray dropped the rope and hurried down using the niches that angled through the V that formed the last few feet of the climb to the cliff dwelling. As he went he pictured the ancient ones, men, children and women with baskets upon their heads, carrying loads to their sky home. When he lost his grip with one toe, he found himself hanging from his arms only. Ray regained his footing and forced himself to slow down. If he fell, Dylan would be forced into making some tough choices.

He heard the whirring motor of a drone. The

flying camera appeared a moment later, looking like a mechanical dragonfly. He did not pause as he continued down the wooden log ladder. The drone hovered, tilted, sank. Then it swooped close to the man that the riflemen shot in the head. Ray did not know if the drone had a microphone but Dylan was speaking to it and using gestures that Jack could interpret and that Agent Forrest likely could, as well. Those gestures had been the way to communicate with other tribes in the southwest when they did not share a common language. Ray's education had included learning these signs and now he was grateful for that. Dylan explained that they needed medical assistance and that the man at the foot of the cliff had been killed by the armed men. He pointed up the canyon and told the heartless flying eye which way they went. The drone lifted and zipped up the canyon disappearing from sight as Ray reached the canyon floor.

"Help should be close," said Dylan.

Ray knelt beside Morgan. Her red face frightened him. The color of her cheeks reminded him of the candy apples sold at fairs and rodeos. Was it better that her skin was no longer gray?

"That's the last of my water," said Dylan. "Are you going to make a travois and carry her or wait for Jack?"

"We aren't waiting," said Ray, scooping Morgan up in his arms and heading for his horse. "Cinch him for me. Will you?"

Dylan readied his horse.

"Your body heat will just make her hotter," he warned.

He knew that. But he'd be damned if he'd let her go. He let Dylan lead and then cursed at the slow pace Dylan set. Always the perfectionist, Dylan chose the safest, but not the fastest, route to the spring. At last Ray spotted the lush green of the grasses and reeds that benefitted from year-round water. He handed Morgan down to Dylan but caught up with him before he reached the spring and relieved him of his precious cargo.

"I won't drop her," Dylan promised.

Ray needed to get Morgan cooled. He splashed into the gurgling water muddying the hole. The horses did not care. They had followed and were now pawing at the mud before drinking as horses did. A survival reflex, perhaps to see the area clear of snakes. Ray sat in the water supporting Morgan. Her arms floated out and her dark hair billowed up around her head. He kept her down so that only her face and hands broke the surface. There he waited, keeping an eye on her.

Thank God this canyon had a spring. Most were dry and he knew what would have happened then. Morgan's blood would have grown thicker and thicker as the dry air stole more moisture from her skin and lungs. Then her organs would fail. First her kidneys and liver and finally her heart. That beautiful, kind and willing heart.

"Morgan, darling," he whispered. "Come back to me. Come back, sweetheart. I love you. Let me have just one chance to prove it to you."

Dylan stood with the horses, watching Ray hold the weightless woman who floated like a water spirit.

"Stay," he whispered. "For Lisa and for me. We need you."

Her fingers moved, curling and then extending. Her limp body regained a more natural muscle tone. His breathing was fast now, nearly as fast as hers. Morgan's eyelids fluttered and this time he saw her beautiful brown eyes as she gazed up at the sky.

"Ahh," she said and lifted an index finger.

He followed the direction of her gaze and saw a hot air balloon with a blue, yellow and red chevron pattern followed by one that was shaped like a gigantic butterfly and a third that resembled the head of the blue Cheshire cat.

She smiled, following the floating parade with only her eyes. Her hand dropped back into the spring water.

"Morgan? Sweetheart?" Ray kept one hand on the middle of her back and swept the hair from her forehead. "Can you hear me?"

Her gaze shifted to him and a line formed between her brows. Confusion or disappointment? He was not certain but she continued to stare.

"Ray?"

"Yes!" He laughed. He had been so afraid the heat would damage her brain, sending her into that spiral from which there was no return.

"Lisa?" She struggled now to get her feet under her with clumsy, weak thrashing.

"Lie still. Lisa is safe. She's with the FBI. Remember?"

"The men." She continued to struggle, so Ray eased her up, dragging her onto his lap.

Dylan left him and the horses who continued to suck up the water in noisy slurps. Ray listened and heard the four-wheelers but the reeds and high green grass blocked his view of their approach. He heard them pause and heard Dylan speaking but could not make out what was said over the engine noise.

"They're gone," said Ray. "The man who took you is gone, too."

"Dead," she said and pinched her eyes closed. She pressed a hand to her forehead. "They said you…worked for them."

He scowled. He wasn't working for the ones the FBI were chasing. Was this some delusion her confused mind had created?

The motors revved and the four-wheelers moved on. Dylan reappeared.

"Didn't you tell them we need help?" asked Ray.

Dylan gave him a certain look that Ray read as annoyance.

"I did but they barely slowed down. Seems catching those men is a higher priority."

Ray seethed. Morgan had put her faith in those agents and they had failed to keep her safe, had endangered her life, been too slow to get to her and now they left her here when just one of those four-wheelers could bring her into town in less than an hour.

"I'm glad I didn't take the test," said Dylan.

"What test?"

"They recruited me after I left the service. And a few times after that."

"You never told me that," said Ray.

Morgan lifted her hands to brush back her short crop of hair. She looked so different with her bangs swept back to reveal her high forehead and widow's peak.

"How do you feel?"

"Dizzy. Nauseous. I'm trying not to puke."

Her color had changed from hot pink to a greenish gray. Ray had seen enough in Iraq to recognize a person who was at risk of going into shock. He wanted to give her water, but was afraid. He knew she needed to be conscious and the shock dictated against letting her drink.

"Horses," said Dylan. His friend disappeared through the grass.

Ray leaned in and kissed Morgan's cheek. "You have to stick with me. You're strong. Stay awake."

"Vision is funny…like looking down a hole."

Tunnel vision. Her body began to grow slack again as she slipped into the swoon.

"Morgan!" He shook her. Her head lolled forward and against his chest. He had to get her to a hospital. Ray stood, still holding her in his arms, and charged out of the spring to find three horsemen: Jack, tribal police chief Tinnin and Jack's younger brother, Kurt Bear Den. Kurt was a paramedic for the air ambulance, and Ray had never been so glad to see a person in his life.

Kurt was already off his horse and reaching for his bag.

"Put her there," Kurt ordered, motioning to the shady side of the canyon.

Within short order, Kurt had Morgan's arm sterilized and an IV inserted. Ray didn't know what was in the clear sack of fluid that Kurt ordered him to hold in the air. All that mattered was that it was moving from the transparent bag and into Morgan's body. Ray lifted his head to the sky and began to sing a prayer for the return of Morgan's spirit to him.

Above, the messenger to the creator circled on the currents of air.

The golden eagle was back, soaring with his prayers.

Chapter Twenty-Four

Morgan woke in the ambulance and again as they loaded her into the helicopter. Later on, she recalled the emergency room with the blinding white lights and the headache that shot pain behind her eyes.

"I'm her husband."

She knew that voice. But she did not have a husband. *Ray. Of course.* He was so good at lying she almost believed him. Almost believed he cared. Almost believed she would have married him. Almost.

Somehow her past and the deceptions of Lisa's father had taught her nothing.

Her legs cramped and the pain made her cry out. Someone gripped her hand.

"I'm here, Morgan."

Her body ached as if she had the flu. This time when the dizziness came she welcomed it, throwing herself into the darkness to escape the torment of her body.

When she woke again she was lying as still as a corpse with her hands carefully placed on either side of her body, which was draped in a white bedsheet. Above her head a muted light shone down on her. Her body felt cold and something moved beneath her, like water.

For a moment she thought she was on a slab in the morgue.

The sounds flooded in next, followed by the beep of the machine that recorded her heartbeat and the noise from the corridor outside her room. She breathed out her relief.

She had been in a hospital bed once before, after Lisa was born. She had delivered her child herself, alone, in the studio apartment in Tucson. Then called the ambulance because she was afraid for Lisa. Her last visit to the hospital had been the final time she had seen her father. What would he say if he knew what his deed had caused?

The tears slid down her cheeks and she smiled. She could cry again. That meant she was no longer dry as the desiccated bodies of those who venture into the arid wilds without enough water.

Now she heard the sound of a pump and then the sensation of movement beneath her again. Some kind of cooling pad, she decided and closed her eyes. She moved just her arms, bending them to lace her fingers over her middle and the machine beside her started to wail.

She glanced at the upright IV. She shifted and felt the tug that told her she had both a catheter and something else down there beneath the clean white sheets. She winced and something like a growl escaped her.

She caught movement to her left and shifted her gaze. Two men stood in a silhouette against the blue glass of the window. They stepped forward into the light. Ray Strong and Detective Jack Bear Den, she realized.

"Keep that arm straight, darlin'," said Ray.

Darling. She smiled and complied then closed her eyes. Was she his darling? That was good, wasn't it? But no. Her smile ebbed. He brushed away the trails of the tears that fell from the corners of her eyes to soak into the hair at her temples. His touch was so gentle and so sincere, or was that just her trying to see only what she wished to see instead of what was.

She opened her eyes and stared up at Ray.

With Lisa's father, her love had been as foolish and childish and immature as the bud of a rose. An infatuation that would not have lasted even if he had been all he had claimed. But for Ray she had the love of a woman, full and lush and blooming. Despite what she knew of him and his flaws, she had tumbled into a love so strong that it ached to look at him. But now she was faced with a terrible choice. She could love him and protect him, even from his friend who was a detective. Or she could love him and do what was right for her tribe and reveal what he was, a man working for BEAR.

"Hi," said Ray, lifting her hand as if she were made of glass. She felt like that, somehow. Fragile with a heart cold and yet still beating. "You gave us all a scare. But you're doing better. And your core temperature is dropping." He motioned to one of the monitors. Then he drew up a chair and sat on the edge.

Core temperature? She shifted and decided that was one of the intrusions she felt.

Ray seemed so concerned and attentive. She stared at his handsome face. The money was gone. So why was he still here?

Hope flared like a shooting star and just as quickly winked out. The words of her abductor bubbled up like road tar. *"Your boyfriend was working for us all along. You really think we'd leave you for the FBI to question without knowing what your dad told you?"*

She looked at him and wondered if she could just pretend. Pretend she didn't know he had deceived her. Pretend he would stay. Her gaze shifted to the form looming behind Ray. Detective

Bear Den loomed like a menacing dark angel, his thick brows sinking over his green eyes.

"I'd like..." She stopped speaking because her voice was nearly unrecognizable, just the scratching of dry sticks against each other, more rasp than speech.

"Just rest," said Ray. "You're safe. Lisa's safe. I'm so relieved. I was afraid I was going to lose you there."

Either Ray was deceiving her or someone close to him was using him. *Our man*, Gifford had said. Who was close enough to Ray that he would trust him implicitly? Her gaze turned to Detective Jack Bear Den, his grim visage now suddenly seemed a threat.

"Water," she said.

"Not yet. They said they have to be sure you are fully conscious." Ray lifted the call button someone had tied to the raised rail of her bed and depressed the plastic button. In a few minutes, the nurse appeared. Her gray hair was pulled back from her fleshy face and her hot-pink top was covered with Disney princesses in a rosy color repeated in her scrub bottoms and again with her rubber-soled clogs, also pink. Her stethoscope dangled from her pocket and held her ID card.

"Well, look who's awake," said the nurse. "I'm Kathy. We met when you came on my floor."

Morgan didn't remember. Kathy asked the men to step out. Ray refused.

The nurse put her hands on her wide hips and made a face but seem resigned. It seemed to Morgan that they had had this conversation before.

"Ray, please," Morgan whispered.

His eyes widened and his expression changed to something close to pain. She felt the stab of guilt. He was tired, dirty and needed a shave. His clothing was rumpled and he had circles under his eyes. He looked as if he'd been dragged all the way down the canyon behind his horse. But what she saw most clearly was the shock of her wanting his absence.

"Just for a minute," she said, her voice still not seeming her own.

He pressed his lips together and nodded. Then he trailed his friend from the room.

Here was her chance. She could ask the nurse to call Luke Forrest and tell him all that Gifford had told her. She could point her finger at Ray and tell them that he was no better than her father, helping those extremists. Or she could trust her heart.

That heart had been wrong before and disappointed so often. She barely had the courage to listen. But she closed her eyes and tried. And there it was. Against reason and against evidence to the contrary, she believed in Ray and what that horrible man had said changed nothing. She loved

Ray and she would give him his due. Love and trust were two inseparable entities. You could not have one without the other.

Kathy checked the monitors and listened to Morgan's heart. Then she raised the bed so Morgan was sitting up.

"Your husband is as stubborn as a potbellied pig I once owned," said Kathy.

"My husband?"

The nurse glanced toward the empty door. "I knew it." She turned pale blue eyes back on Morgan. "Between the FBI and that detective and Mr. Strong, I just didn't have the energy." She snorted. "He's cute though and very devoted to you. I think he'd like to be your husband. You could do worse. That's certain."

Kathy returned her attention to her patient. When she finished, Morgan had been thoroughly mauled but she now had nothing but the IV and heart monitors attached to her body.

"They won't tell me anything, of course. No one ever does. But I have to tell you that I could not get that other one, Mr. Strong, to leave the room. My friend in the ER said that he was impossible in the ER and ignored the Critical Care Unit ICC rules about visiting hours."

"How long have I been here?" asked Morgan.

She glanced at a digital watch with a wide pink strap. "You came in yesterday and onto my floor a few hours ago. It's 5:00 p.m. on Tuesday and you're in Phoenix."

"Phoenix?" She had assumed she was in the small community hospital in Darabee.

"Yep. If you are in pain, I can give you something," said the nurse.

Morgan shook her head. This was not the sort of pain she wanted numbed. It was more a confusion over her feelings for Ray. She knew his reputation and what he thought of himself. But that man and the man she knew were two different people. She drew a breath, filling her lungs with sweet cool air and a sense of hopeful optimism that most would think foolish and others would call reckless. She wanted to tell Ray how she felt and see if she could convince him to stay with her and Lisa, to see if they might grow into a family.

"I need to speak to Ray. Alone,"

The nurse paused and lifted her thin brows.

"I do not want the detective or the FBI back in here," said Morgan.

Her nurse could not have been much over five feet tall but the iron in her expression and the confidence in her smile made Morgan believe that she was up for that challenge.

"I'll have that detective get some ice chips. You have FBI outside your door, too. They might be able to hear you talking."

Kathy offered Morgan ice water from a plastic

cup with a straw. Nothing had ever been quite as welcome as that first sip. It soothed her raw throat. She felt it glide down her esophagus and all the way to her stomach.

"Slow at first," said Kathy. "Let's see how that sits."

It seemed to arrive in her stomach like moisture to a dry sponge. She felt no discomfort so Kathy let her have the rest.

"You've had a lot of intravenous fluid, so you should be feeling much better. Are you hungry?"

Morgan nodded.

"I'll see about getting you something to eat. I have lemon ice at my station. Best start with that."

Kathy spun with military efficiency and reversed course past the empty bed beside Morgan's and out the door. Her voice was clear as she ordered Jack Bear Den to follow her.

A moment later, Ray appeared, peeking in at her and then casting her a welcome smile that was as cheerful as a spring bouquet. His eyes sparkled and the smile masked the fatigue on his features.

"How you feeling?"

She motioned him forward, causing the IV in her arm to throb. He moved to her side and took hold of her hand, his thumb stroking her skin. The tingle that followed the simple touch was unexpected and as welcome as July rain.

"That man who took me?" she whispered in Tonto Apache.

Ray's smile vanished and he looked suddenly forbidding and fierce.

"He's dead, Morgan. He can't hurt you ever again."

"I know. I saw those men kill him."

Now his thick brows sank low over his dark eyes. "You saw them?"

"Did they catch them?"

He shook his head and leaned closer, matching her quiet tones. "No. The FBI pursued them to the end of the canyon. They found a lean-to with their horses and a half-full plastic water trough for their livestock but no sign of the men. They asked Jack to go up there with Chief Tinnin to have a look. Best they can figure from the tracks and the spikes they found was that those two had a hot-air balloon waiting. With it, they just drifted up into the hot-air-balloon festival and floated to Phoenix with the rest of the participants.

"Could you identify them?" asked Ray.

She shook her head. "They wore gloves and masks."

His shoulders sagged with visible relief. "Thank God."

"The one who took me."

"Gifford Journey," Ray spat the name. Then he

called him a name that made Morgan's ears heat. "May he find no peace in the grave."

"He wanted me to show him where we put the money," she said.

"That's what they wanted, wasn't it? The FBI? To use you to get to them. You could have died." Ray's face flushed and his free hand gripped the bed rail so tight his knuckles turned white.

He'd been against her working with the FBI. She'd shut him out. She hadn't trusted him and as a result she'd almost left her precious daughter an orphan. She might have been just like Ray had been, alone, vulnerable and left to the tribe to place.

"I'm so sorry, Ray."

He sank to his knees. "No. Don't be. You're safe. Lisa is safe."

"But they didn't catch them. It was all for nothing."

"They have their horses. Maybe some physical evidence. They have the Gifford connection. He'll lead them somewhere. They've called in his father, Renzo Journey, for questioning. His father owns a stone and gravel business in Carefree."

Now Morgan squeezed Ray's hand. The weariness dragged on her as her body demanded rest. But she had to tell him the rest.

"Ray, the man who took me, he said that they had a man on the inside. He called him 'our man.'"

Ray loomed over her. For just a moment she reconsidered telling him what Gifford had said to her. What if the inside man was Ray?

"Where?" Everything about him had turned hard and dangerous.

She swallowed back her trepidation but her heart monitor betrayed her, beating at a faster pace. It was not too late to turn back, but she wouldn't. She had to know the truth.

"I don't know who. He just said, *'Our man.'* He said something like that you could be trusted because 'their man' told them to trust you."

"Me?" He pointed a finger to his chest. "I could be trusted?" He glanced past the empty bed beside her to the open door. "We have to tell Jack," said Ray.

Morgan shook her head. "What if it's him, the one they called our man?"

Ray's eyes narrowed. She knew what he was thinking. He trusted Jack with his life. But Morgan barely knew him.

"It's not Jack."

"How do you know?"

"The same way you know it's not me."

She stared at him in silence as her skin prickled with apprehension.

"What else did he say?"

"That you had been working for them all along. And that they were not stupid enough to leave me alive to talk to the FBI without knowing everything my father had told me first."

His eyes widened and his mouth dropped open for a moment before he clamped it shut so tight the muscles at his cheeks bulged. Then he took a step closer before pausing to glance back at the door. In the hallway, his friend Jack waited with the FBI agent stationed to guard her.

"Morgan, I'm not the inside man and if they have one, I don't know who it is." He waited in total stillness as she met his gaze.

She didn't have any special powers to divine the truth. She knew only that she wanted to believe him. But her daughter's safety was also at stake. That made her hesitate.

"I know that you have had some men lie to you, trick you and even use you. Kenshaw Little Falcon did ask me to discover what you knew of your father's dealings with the eco-extremists. He's my shaman, Morgan. I'm sorry if I hurt you."

She wanted, no longed, to believe him.

"I don't know what to do."

"Believe me," he begged. "Believe in me. You won't be sorry."

She wouldn't survive it, another deception, because this time she knew that she loved Ray foolishly and totally. If he broke her heart, there would be nothing left. Before, with that married man who had deceived her, it was her pride that had suffered. She had lost an infatuation and a fantasy. Now she faced much greater stakes. If she didn't believe him, she would lose him. If she did believe him and he was deceiving her, she would lose him, too.

She nodded. "What should we do?"

His eyes closed and he placed his hand over them rubbing outward as if to eradicate the memory of this near miss.

"You believe me?" he asked.

"I do."

He lifted his head from his hands and watched her. "Why?"

She couldn't tell him it was because she loved him. She knew Ray was fond of her and was attracted to her. But neither of those meant that he loved her or that he planned to stick around after this was over.

Morgan cleared her throat and went halfway there. "I believe you because I believe my heart. I have to."

He leaned forward, pressing his forehead to hers. "Thank you. I'll see that you never regret it."

"But if you didn't know, then that means someone very close to you is using you."

The growl began in Ray's throat and leaped out as a roar.

"Jack!" he bellowed.

"No, wait," she said. But it was too late because

the big man entered at a fast walk, one hand on his pistol as he swept the room for signs of a threat.

If Ray was wrong and Jack was the inside man, then Morgan was now facing the person that the eco-extremists had placed on the inside.

Chapter Twenty-Five

Morgan blew out a breath, refusing to let the fear gobble her up. She had to trust Ray's belief in Jack because if she didn't, this nightmare might never end.

And once it did, well then she could keep Ray.

Morgan sank back in her bedding. That was it. Her stupid, deluded attempt to keep Ray meant that she couldn't ever be safe. Because once she was, his mission from their shaman was complete and he could leave her.

Morgan squeezed her eyes shut, ashamed at the coward she had become.

Ray met Jack at the door and the two stepped out in the hall before her door. She could hear outside Ray's voice speaking Tonto Apache and Jack's reply, a low gruff whisper. What were they saying?

She needed to tell her tribal police everything. Tell the FBI everything. Help them catch these men, whose plans were unknown but involved a great deal of explosives. Then she would get Lisa back and have to tell Ray goodbye.

The nurse came and went, bringing a tray with Italian lemon ice, gelatin, coffee and apple juice. Morgan closed her eyes to savor that first spoonful of ice.

"How's that?" asked her nurse.

"Mmmm… Thank you."

"I'd like to have you take a walk around the floor in a little while."

"Sounds good."

The nurse promised to order her some real food and left, passing Ray at the foot of the empty bed beside Morgan's. Behind him came Detective Bear Den. Morgan told the detective just what she had related to Ray.

Jack Bear Den cleared his throat. "If it's not you, Ray, or me, then there are only two other possibilities."

"Dylan and Kenshaw Little Falcon," said Ray. "It can't be Dylan."

Jack nodded. "I agree. But if it is not Dylan, then it means that our shaman and the leader of Tribal Thunder is working for these extremists and it's my duty to arrest him."

"I need to speak to field agent Forrest," said Morgan.

"Already on his way," said Bear Den. The detective glanced to Ray. "I've got to go. This is my best shot to bring him in before the FBI gets to him. If they take him while he's not on reservation land, I might never get a chance to get to the bottom of this."

Ray nodded and Jack turned to Morgan. "Thank you for your help, Morgan. I'll be in touch."

Ray walked him out but returned in a few minutes and took a seat beside her bed.

"You're staying here?" she asked.

"Until I know you're safe."

"But the man who sent you to watch over me might be the man they're all after. In which case, you don't have any obligation to stay here with me."

"You're wrong there."

"Am I?"

He nodded.

"Why are you staying?"

"Because you still need me."

Morgan's mouth twisted at that. This was not the answer she longed to hear.

"I'm not your responsibility anymore. The FBI is protecting me now."

He leaned forward in the chair at the side of her bed and gave her a long, hard stare. "Are you asking me to leave?"

"No."

"Good. Because I'm not going. Not anytime soon."

She told her foolishly thrumming heart that Ray

was staying out of some sense of honor. Not love, she reminded herself.

"If Kenshaw did what you claim, he'll answer for it. But he was right about one thing. You need someone to watch over you and for now, that someone is me."

THE FBI HAD not wanted Morgan to leave her room but she had been up to use the bathroom a few times. Dinner had helped give her some much needed energy. Ray said the color was coming back to her cheeks.

That evening Dylan appeared with a change of clothing for Ray and some other necessities. His mother had also sent Morgan a simple two-piece camp dress for her to wear home. All Apache camp dresses consisted of a loose long-sleeved blouse and modest ankle-length skirt. The outfit was cool cotton and colorful. This one was royal blue and had a lemon-yellow rickrack on both yoke and which repeated around the skirt.

"She'd heard about what happened and wanted Morgan to have something clean for the journey home. This was my sister's. She wore it when she was mentoring Paula Fields on her sunrise ceremony."

It was a very thoughtful gift.

"That's nice. We'll see it gets back to your mom."

"I'll bring it in to her, all right?"

Ray trusted Dylan to keep watch over Morgan while he stepped out for a few minutes.

"I've never seen him like this," said Dylan.

"Like what?" asked Morgan.

Dylan grinned. "In love, Morgan. Hasn't he told you?"

Her heartbeat blipped louder on the monitor as she shook her head in denial.

"You're wrong, Dylan. He is just worried about me."

Dylan's boyish grin remained. "If you say so."

"Knock. Knock," said a male voice from outside the room. A moment later field agent Luke Forrest entered with his partner, Cassidy Cosen.

Dylan lifted his phone and called Ray who appeared before Forrest had finished the pleasantries of asking how Morgan was feeling. Cassidy told her that Lisa was well and passed on a letter from her.

"I have a daughter. She just turned thirteen," said Agent Cosen.

Thirteen was an important age for Apache girls and Morgan knew Cassidy Cosen's daughter was Black Mountain Apache. Some of Morgan's friends had even attended her daughter's sunrise ceremony because the invitations had been sent far and wide.

Morgan accepted the letter with thanks and was reading the contents when Ray reappeared. She finished and pressed the page to her chest over her heart.

"Can I speak to her?" Morgan asked Agent Forrest.

"You can see her," said Luke. "Just as soon as you're released, which we think will be tomorrow."

"What about protection?" asked Ray.

"Not necessary. We have credible intel that Morgan and Lisa are no longer in danger."

"What intel?" asked Dylan.

"I'm afraid I'm not at liberty to say. But we believe that the men Morgan met in the canyon are satisfied that Morgan is ignorant of their identity and does not know who hired her father to murder Sanchez."

Agent Cosen spoke up. "That means she does not need our protection or the US Marshals Service to provide witness protection. She's not a witness to anything and her father wisely told her nothing."

Forrest took over. "All of the money has been recovered and we have advised the public of this with a press conference. You can see it on the local news again at eleven."

"What about the police in Darabee? Chief Rowe can't have been alone over there," asked Dylan.

"Very good, Mr. Tehauno. I really was serious

about recommending you for the FBI. I wish you'd consider my suggestion to apply."

Ray's friend flushed and nodded.

"To answer your question," said Cassidy Cosen, "it's an ongoing investigation. We can't discuss that. But we can say that we are as certain as possible that it is safe for Ms. Hooke to go home. We'll keep the agent here overnight as a courtesy and escort her back to Turquoise Canyon tomorrow."

"Are you still using her as bait?" said Ray.

"Absolutely not," said Forrest.

Ray and Dylan exchanged a look and Ray nodded his acceptance of the FBI's assurances.

Morgan waited for either Dylan Tehauno or Ray to mention their suspicions about Kenshaw Little Falcon. She would not be the first. Accusing a man of such a thing was serious but made more so by the fact that he was a fellow tribe member. She knew that tribal matters were often handled by the tribal courts and Detective Bear Den was on his way to speak to him. It was rare that a member of their tribe was turned over to the state for prosecution and she could not think of one instance where a tribe member was given to federal custody.

The FBI departed and Morgan asked Ray about it.

"I'm giving Jack time to speak to Kenshaw.

We'll let the Feds know in the morning and I'll be here until then."

She had Ray for one more night and she was going to be spending it in a hospital bed. What a waste.

Morgan made a promise to herself. The next time she and Ray were alone, she would reveal her true feelings. He had told her that he was not the kind of man to settle down. Morgan prepared to have her heart broken once more but her fears would not muzzle her because the only thing more frightening than telling Ray that she loved him was not telling him.

Chapter Twenty-Six

Ray spoke with Luke Forrest the following morning in the hallway outside Morgan's room while she met with the nurse to sign her release papers. Forrest informed him that Gifford's father, Renzo Journey, was a suspect and under FBI surveillance. "He didn't send his son after Morgan, but we are fairly sure that Gifford got his information from his father and then acted alone."

"How did the other men in BEAR find out what Gifford was up to, then?"

"We believe that Renzo notified them."

Ray digested that. The FBI believed that Renzo had turned over his own son to BEAR. He must have known what would happen. He glanced at Forrest. The lowered brow and the perfect clarity of his expression told Ray that was exactly what had happened.

"I'd never turn over my own son," said Ray. Not that he had a son. He glanced toward Morgan's room and wondered briefly if she wanted more children. Lisa was fast becoming a teenager. Her daughter would be more like an auntie than a sibling. Changing diapers while raising a teenager wouldn't be easy. Ray rubbed his neck.

"Strong?"

He turned his attention back to Forrest.

"I was saying that Morgan is in no danger."

"How can you be sure of that?"

"Not at—"

Ray finished the familiar refrain. "Liberty to say. I know." Ray scrubbed his knuckles over the stubble on his jaw. "Well you won't mind if I stick around awhile to be sure."

"Gifford is dead. The money is gone. A representative of BEAR told her that she's safe. What do you want, a certificate? You're done, Ray. I'm sure your shaman will tell you the same. Go home."

That was just it. He didn't have a home. He had a trailer up near the lake. He had a tribe and friends and the Yeagers who treated him like a son. But until he'd met Morgan, he had not realized that he did not have a home. And he wanted one. With her. Trouble was he had no cause to stick around.

He knew Kenshaw would tell him to lay off it, if Jack hadn't arrested their shaman.

"What about Jefferson Rowe?" asked Ray.

"Awaiting trial. He can't hurt her."

Ray wondered about one other threat. Ironically, it was the very same man who had sent him to Morgan. Worse, he was a fellow member of their tribe. Ray was not going to point the finger at his shaman and the leader of Tribal Thunder no matter what Jack thought Kenshaw had done.

But what if not speaking endangered Morgan?

"What?" asked Forrest.

"Detective Bear Den had some concerns about…" Ray could not believe he was doing this. But if Kenshaw was dirty, he did not deserve protection. And Ray disagreed with Jack on one matter. Jack wanted to keep housecleaning on site. While Ray thought they might need an outside contractor.

"Concerned about?" echoed field agent Forrest.

"About how much inside information Kenshaw Little Falcon has on BEAR and WOLF."

"Concerns?" Forrest's impatience morphed into a look that showed apprehensions of his own.

"Kenshaw sent his brother down to Lilac to fetch his niece before the Lilac mass shooting. He sent me to Morgan just before it became known that her father hid all that money."

"Why don't you let us handle that?"

"Too late. Jack is still angry that he lost his twin brother, Carter, to witness protection. He said he's going to arrest our shaman and bring him to tribal police for questioning."

Luke Forrest had his phone out before Ray had even finished speaking.

"He can't," said Forrest.

"Why not?"

Forrest pressed his lips closed. He lifted his phone and used it to point at the agent guarding Morgan's door. "Gutherie will see you to the border of the reservation." Then he stalked away. Ray heard him issuing orders into his phone. He caught two words—*cover* and *blown*.

His brows lifted. Was Kenshaw working with the FBI? That, however, did not explain how he knew the plans of BEAR and WOLF before anyone else. It did explain why the FBI would want him as an informant.

Ray recalled that in February, after the shooting, Kenshaw and Carter Bear Den had been detained for questioning. Carter had gone into protection. Kenshaw had been released. Now he understood why. And Jack was going to arrest Kenshaw. That would certainly jeopardize any future intel Kenshaw might provide. And it might also endanger Kenshaw's life.

Ray lifted his phone and dialed. Jack picked up on the second ring.

"What?" asked Jack.

"Where are you?"

"Eating breakfast with Kurt at Mom's. Why?"

"You see Kenshaw?"

"Missed him last night. But I know where he'll be today," said Ray.

"Don't go."

"What? Why?"

"Trust me. Leave it for now. I'll explain when I get up there."

Ray heard a chiming tone.

"I got another call," said Jack. There was a pause. "It's Forrest."

"Take it. Call me back."

"Okay." The line went dead.

Ray pictured Jack in his mother's kitchen, putting two and two together. He wondered if Jack had ever sent in that sibling DNA test. Jack had told him that Carter had furnished a cheek swab. That was all he needed to learn for certain if he and his brothers shared the same father. Ray knew Carter and Jack's mother, Annetta, very well. He could not picture the special education teacher cheating on her husband. And the chances of getting pregnant with twins, each by a different father had to be astronomical. But not impossible, Jack had told him. And Jack looked different from any of the other three boys. Carter, Kurt and Tommy were nearly interchangeable in looks, size and personality. But Jack had always been different.

Ray thought about Annetta Bear Den again and decided that you never really knew a person.

The nurse left Morgan's room holding her clipboard. She nodded as she passed him. Ray found Morgan dressed and standing by the bed. He paused to take in the sight of Morgan dressed in so traditional a manner. The bright blue complemented her skin and the bands of pieced yellow fabric triangles formed a yoke at her neck. The bands repeated twice more on the skirt.

He switched to Tonto because it seemed right. "You look beautiful."

Her smile lit him up inside and out. He stepped closer and she slipped naturally into his arms.

"I can't wait to get home and see Lisa," said Morgan. "I know she is okay. But she's never been away from home overnight and I just won't feel right until I see her with my own eyes."

He knew that when she had been in danger, he'd had reason not to let Morgan out of his sight. But now? The FBI said she was safe. She didn't need him.

But what about him, about them?

Had there ever been a them, or was all that he felt and all that he longed for only what he wanted?

He had no doubts that Morgan deserved better than the likes of him. If he really loved her, he would let her go. Then Morgan would be free to find the sort of responsible, caring man who would make her a fine husband and good father for her girl. Upstanding, decent. A man like Jack or Dylan or the kind of man Hatch would have been.

Of course, Jack was too serious. Lord, did he ever laugh or crack a joke? Dylan was too predictable and upstanding to the point that he never did seem to make a mistake. And Hatch, well he was dead, so whatever kind of husband he might have made was lost in that distant blood-soaked sand.

Somehow he needed to do what was best for Lisa and for Morgan. He didn't know how he would say goodbye without making a fool of himself. But he was going to try, because he loved Morgan and he wanted her to have the best. He knew only one thing with certainty—that was not him.

THE DRIVE BACK to Turquoise Canyon was uncomfortable. Morgan felt by turns as if she were traveling with a stranger and also someone too preoccupied to even notice her presence. He was preparing himself to leave her. She felt it with the same keenness she had the IV that had punctured her vein.

Morgan had been told that Lisa would be returned late in the day to her home. She wanted to be certain that she was there in time to meet her. Cookie was with Lisa, so when she opened the front door to her home, the house felt empty and far too quiet.

Ray followed her in, checking each room before returning to her where she waited in the kitchen. The look he cast her made her breath catch, for it was full of longing and heat and a pain that she had only glimpsed before. Now it was there, clear and tangible as an electrical storm. He was summoning the strength to leave her. While she needed to gather the courage to make him stay.

"I believe you'll be safe now, Morgan," he said.

"You've done your duty to your shaman and to me," she said, but it wasn't enough. She wanted more. And all she had to do to get it was risk everything by telling him that she was madly, hopelessly and foolishly in love with him.

"Do you need anything else from me?"

She stepped closer, her mouth dry and her palms damp. "Yes."

His brow rose and he cocked his head as he watched her advance in small hesitant steps. She lifted her arms and looped them about his neck. He grasped her waist but she could not tell if he meant to pull her in or push her away.

"I need you, Ray Strong."

He flushed. "You mean you want me to sleep with you?"

"Yes. Every night."

Now his eyes went wide as her meaning began to sink in.

"What about Lisa?" he asked.

"She needs a father."

Now he did let go and backed toward the kitchen door, which was the closest exit. With each step he shook his head in denial.

"Ray, if you don't want me. If you don't love me, then you should go. But if you are leaving because of some sense that you are not capable of being a husband and a father, I have hard news. You have been that to us already."

"I haven't even known you two weeks."

"It's enough for me to be sure that you are the one I've waited for all my life."

He pressed his big callused hands to his mouth and squeezed his eyes shut. Gradually he lowered his hands and straightened his shoulders. Then he opened his eyes and met her gaze. The pain was still there, making his eyes glassy.

"It's not me, Morgan. You were under attack. You were alone. So it's natural to turn to a protector. But you're confusing your need with love."

"I'm not confused, Ray. I know what I feel."

"Are you forgetting that I deceived you?"

"You kept your word to our shaman. You did what he asked. I have secrets, too, Ray. I never told anyone but you about Lisa's father because the truth made me feel stupid and used. You are entitled to your secrets. Everyone is. It doesn't change my feelings."

"I'm not husband material. I've been arrested. I've served time. If not for Jack and Dylan getting me help, I would have been dishonorably discharged from the US Marines. I don't deserve you or Lisa."

"Because you switched seats in that convoy with Hatch Yeager?"

His mouth dropped open and then snapped shut. But he found his voice had abandoned him. It was as if she had shot an arrow right to the heart of the matter.

"I forgive you in Yeager's place. He would forgive you and want you to forgive yourself. It was a prank, Ray. You could not have known what would happen."

"Of course I could. We were in a hot spot. They called that place the Triangle of Death."

She stepped forward and pressed an open palm over his heart, feeling the steady beat in his chest.

"You have been nothing but tender and protective to my daughter. You have been nothing but conscientious and loving toward me. I refuse to believe that you did that as part of your assignment. You have feelings for me, Ray. I know it. And you are allowed to be happy. Allowed to make me happy because you did not die back there. And because you did not die, you have to live with your regrets. But you have to live."

"What if I screw this up, too?" he asked.

She smiled as she realized that he was considering it and it scared him to death.

"Your past makes you who you are, Ray. You're not the kid who joined the US Marines or the man who drank too much and flipped his vehicle outside Darabee. You're the man who protected me, rescued me…loved me. Don't let us go because it scares you, Ray. Be brave. Be the risk taker you claim to be and claim me."

He hesitated one instant more as his gaze swept her face, reading her expression. Did he see the love in her eyes, the willingness in her smile and feel the hope in her heart?

Ray could barely breathe past the hope that rose in his throat. Morgan really believed he could do this. He'd taken so many chances, survived so many foolish risks. But this chance, this risk would involve a child and a good woman. Did she understand what she was asking?

He held her gaze and Morgan nodded. "You can, Ray. If you want to."

The lump in his throat remained despite his attempts to swallow it again. Foolish hope, still alive after all this time. Who could have ever predicted that?

"All right. Let's do this."

Then Ray swept Morgan up in an embrace, spinning her once in a circle as she settled against his chest. Their mouths met in a joining that was so much more than physical. In his kiss, she felt the promise of a future together. When he finally set her on her feet, his hands came up to stroke her cheek and glide down her throat before settling on her shoulders. She felt the weight of his hands as he squeezed.

"You sure?" he asked, giving her one more chance to come to her senses. She hoped she never did.

"I am."

He smiled at her. "I love you, Morgan Hooke, and if you'll have me, I want to marry you. I've never been a husband, never had the optimism to consider it, but if you think I can do it, then I'll try every day and night not to let you or Lisa down. Will you be my wife?"

Her reply caught in her throat and all she could manage was a choking sound and a vigorous nod before she threw herself back in his arms, burying her head against his chest. He stroked her head and chuckled.

"Well, I'd cry at the prospect of marrying me, too."

She slapped him on the shoulder, that same shoulder that held the tattoo of an eagle, a tattoo he'd gotten in the hopes that someday he would be able to see beyond the obvious. Now he felt that he saw farther than ever before. He saw possibilities and a future with this woman and her child. And if he looked very far indeed, he saw more children in the home they would make together.

* * * * *

There is more trouble brewing on Turquoise Canyon as Apache hotshot and war hero Dylan Tehauno saves wealthy documentary filmmaker Charlotte Wrangler from a wildfire, only to find they've been framed for arson and murder. On the run from the killers and the law and battling the fire of attraction burning between them, Dylan and Charlotte must uncover the evidence that will prove their innocence.

Jenna Kernan's APACHE PROTECTOR: TRIBAL THUNDER *miniseries continues in May 2017 with* HUNTING BOBCAT.

LARGER-PRINT BOOKS!

HARLEQUIN

Presents

PASSION
GUARANTEED
SEDUCTION

GET 2 FREE LARGER-PRINT NOVELS PLUS 2 FREE GIFTS!

WESTERN WP **PROMISES**

YES! Please send me **The Western Promises Collection** in Larger Print. This collection begins with 3 FREE books and 2 FREE gifts (gifts valued at approx. $14.00 retail) in the first shipment, along with the other first 4 books from the collection! If I do not cancel, I will receive 8 monthly shipments until I have the entire 51-book Western Promises collection. I will receive 2 or 3 FREE books in each shipment and I will pay just $4.99 US/ $5.89 CDN for each of the other four books in each shipment, plus $2.99 for shipping and handling per shipment. *If I decide to keep the entire collection, I'll have paid for only 32 books, because 19 books are FREE! I understand that accepting the 3 free books and gifts places me under no obligation to buy anything. I can always return a shipment and cancel at any time. My free books and gifts are mine to keep no matter what I decide.

272 HCN 3070 472 HCN 3070

Name _____ (PLEASE PRINT) _____

Address _____ Apt. # _____

City _____ State/Prov. _____ Zip/Postal Code _____

Signature (if under 18, a parent or guardian must sign)

Mail to the **Reader Service:**
IN U.S.A.: P.O. Box 1867, Buffalo, NY 14240-1867
IN CANADA: P.O. Box 609, Fort Erie, Ontario L2A 5X3

* Terms and prices subject to change without notice. Prices do not include applicable taxes. Sales tax applicable in N.Y. Canadian residents will be charged applicable taxes. This offer is limited to one order per household. All orders subject to approval. Credit or debit balances in a customer's account(s) may be offset by any other outstanding balance owed by or to the customer. Please allow 4 to 6 weeks for delivery. Offer available while quantities last. Offer not available to Quebec residents.

Your Privacy—The Reader Service is committed to protecting your privacy. Our Privacy Policy is available online at www.ReaderService.com or upon request from the Reader Service.

We make a portion of our mailing list available to reputable third parties that offer products we believe may interest you. If you prefer that we not exchange your name with third parties, or if you wish to clarify or modify your communication preferences, please visit us at www.ReaderService.com/consumerschoice or write to us at Reader Service Preference Service, P.O. Box 9062, Buffalo, NY 14240-9062. Include your complete name and address.